STOLEN DREAMS

Other books by Karen Cogan:

The Secret of Castlegate Manor
A Flame in the Wind

STOLEN DREAMS

•

Karen Cogan

AVALON BOOKS
NEW YORK

Published by Thomas Bouregy & Co., Inc.
160 Madison Avenue, New York, NY 10016

Library of Congress Cataloging-in-Publication Data

Cogan, Karen.
    Stolen dreams / Karen Cogan.
        p. cm.
        ISBN 978-0-8034-9847-1 (acid-free paper)
        I. Title.

    PS3603. 0325S76 2007
    813'.6—dc22

                                            2007011968

PRINTED IN THE UNITED STATES OF AMERICA
ON ACID-FREE PAPER
BY HADDON CRAFTSMEN, BLOOMSBURG, PENNSYLVANIA

Dedicated to my husband, John,
the fulfillment of my dreams.

Chapter One

Melinda's pulse quickened as Will reigned Ginger to a halt. She saw his face light up with a warm smile as he looked down at her. She returned his smile and reminded herself that this broad shouldered, sturdy young man was her childhood playmate. In those days, he had been the one schoolmate who had never shunned her when the other children refused to accept a raven-haired Indian girl who had been raised by a white family. It had not been her choice to live in a white man's world. But Will had made it easier.

She squinted into the sun to see his face, shaded by his wide-brimmed hat. He gestured toward her farm and asked, "Are you thawing out from winter?"

"Yes. I'm glad it's over. We lost a few chickens to coyotes and Pa nearly got frostbite bringing in the cows during a blizzard. How about you?"

"We're fine. Lost a few head of cattle, but that's all."

He climbed off the horse and she caught her breath.

1

Though she had seen him at church, she had not realized how tall he had grown. His dark eyes used to be level with hers. Now, he would have to duck to get into the chicken coop.

He fell in step beside her and glanced into her basket. "We've been missing that jam."

"Have you? Then it's good that I'm bringing this to your mother to trade for eggs. We'll be making more jam as soon as the berries get ripe."

"Remember when we used to pick berries together?" His voice carried a wistful tone.

"I remember. We raced to see who could fill the buckets first."

He nodded. "I haven't been out to pick any since the last time I went with you. I've been staying busy around the ranch. Still, I could make time to go picking this summer if you could stand the company."

She wondered if he noticed the pulse beating rapidly in her throat. She must not sound too eager lest she seem too anxious for his attention. She replied evenly, "I'd welcome the company and the help."

He tipped his hat. "I better be gettin' back to work. I gotta work on a fence in the south pasture. But you remember my offer about the berries and let me know when you're going."

Her hunger for his company made her long to extend the conversation. "Maybe I'll see you this week at church. We should be able to get to town."

"I'll look for you after the service."

She nodded, unable to think of anything else to say.

He climbed into the saddle and waved as he turned toward the pasture. She stood a moment, admiring how gracefully he moved, as one with the horse. It reminded her of the times they had ridden to school together. She had felt secure clasping his waist as they rode along.

She remembered how faithfully he had remained her friend. The other children took cues from their parents and made it clear they had no use for a bashful Indian girl. Will, the youngest in a family of five boys, had acquired rugged fists and a resulting reputation that protected him from the taunts any other boy would have received. He looked out for her. No one insulted her within his hearing. But Will did not always hear the ugly comments.

When Ma found out about her treatment, she had taken her out of school to teach her at home. Melinda had not missed the other children. But she had missed Will. Each time Ma sent her the two miles to the Bentley ranch to trade jam for eggs, Melinda had stayed for a chat and glass of lemonade with Will's ma. She had lingered in the hopes that Will would get home from school and she could see him before she had to start home.

Melinda's heart had ached when the awkwardness of adolescence had affected those happy days. For a few years she and Will had become shy with each other, barely speaking when they met. Melinda had deeply mourned the loss of childhood closeness, made especially bitter by the lack of any female playmates. She found escape from the unkind memories by fantasizing that she was an Indian princess, dressed in the finest skins and admired by countless braves. It was a fantasy born of pure imagination since she had seen other Indians only once.

She and Pa were in town when a group of Cheyenne was loaded onto a train for resettlement. They were so bedraggled that she asked Pa what they had done to be punished. Pa hadn't said much, only that they lost a war and were being taken to a new place to live. A shiver stole up her spine at the memory.

Pa didn't like to talk about the Indians. It reminded him of serving in the cavalry, and the way he'd found Melinda. She was the lone survivor after his unit had attacked an unarmed village. He'd found her, frightened and alone, after the commanding officer turned back, leaving Joseph to supervise the burning of the village. He scooped her up and carried her home to Rebecca. Then he'd resigned his commission.

When she was old enough to understand, he told Melinda how she'd come to their family. "It's a terrible thing to see revenge taken on innocent lives," he'd said.

Joseph had no use for vengeance. He and Rebecca had left the outpost and moved to the farm, taking the baby girl with them. Joseph kept a rifle by the door to defend his family and thanked God every night he'd never had to use it. As new settlers moved in, the cavalry chased the remaining Indians onto settlements or sent them fleeing ever farther to the west, leaving Melinda more and more isolated from her heritage.

She often felt caught between two worlds. Yet, now, as she stared after Will, she realized that she could be happy in this world if their relationship could awaken from the cocoon in which it slept. Will had not seemed uneasy when he had spoken to her today. Did she dare to hope that their childhood friendship could be maturing from silkworm to beautiful butterfly? She could think of no other reason that his nearness evoked such a confusion of feelings. The thought brought a flush to her cheeks and a quickening of her pulse.

She composed herself as she walked past the chicken yard and onto the porch. She could hear Will's mother singing as she prepared the noon meal.

Melinda rapped on the door and Hannah greeted her with a smile. "It's good to see you, dear. This has been a long winter. I must be gettin' old. I seem to feel it more than I used to."

Melinda offered the basket of jam. "A coyote got some of our hens and Ma wondered if you could trade for a few eggs."

"Sure. You tell Rebecca you don't have to bring jam every time. We almost always got eggs to spare."

"I'll tell her, but you know Ma. She won't take something for nothing. Besides, we put up lots of jam last summer."

"Come in and sit a bit and tell me about your family while you have a cup of tea."

"The kids were sick over the winter, but they're fine now. All it took was some warm sunshine to set them on their feet," Melinda said.

After they had chatted over their tea, Melinda strolled to the henhouse to gather eggs. As she started home she watched for Will, but he was nowhere to be seen. She tried to convince herself that it was only loneliness for young companionship that made her long to be with him. Yet, she knew it was not so. She would choose him over any young man she had ever met.

A sprinkling of rain fell as she scurried across the meadow. The rich scent of earth mingled with the pungent aroma of pine, filling her senses with the perfume of spring.

She reached home and shook the droplets from her hair. Rebecca looked up with a smile. "Did you get wet?"

"Only a little. I didn't mind."

"I hope we get plenty of rain this spring. We need those fields to produce enough to tide us through next winter. Especially with Daniel growing like a weed and eating everything in sight."

It was true. Her brother had grown several inches over the winter and his appetite had blossomed with his growth. It reminded her of Will and how quickly he had grown into a tall, handsome man.

The week seemed to drag until Sunday finally arrived. Melinda was eager, not only because she missed going to church, but also because it was her next chance to see Will. He sought her out after the service. "We enjoyed the jam. Did you make it yourself?"

"Some of it."

"I bet you cook other things just as well."

"There are a few things I can make."

"Sounds like you're being modest."

"You can decide for yourself if you'd like to come to supper." Melinda sucked in her breath, surprised at herself for her impulsive invitation.

"I'd like that. Is there a time you had in mind?"

"How about tomorrow night? We're having fried chicken. I'm sure an extra guest would be fine as long as I do the cooking."

He grinned. "And I'm sure my Ma would be glad to have my appetite satisfied at your table for a change."

"Ma's feeling that way about Daniel. He eats everything in sight."

When they parted, Melinda debated how to explain the invitation to her parents. Will was an old friend. Would they read more into it? And was there more?

Chapter Two

Melinda fingered the tiny silver heart on her necklace while Joseph drove the wagon into the farmyard. She felt shy to tell her parents about the sudden rekindling of her friendship with Will. She drew in a deep breath as though she could inhale a dose of courage.

Joseph parked the wagon. There would be no better time than now to tell them. "I invited Will to supper tomorrow. I figured I'd do the cooking."

Rebecca exchanged a smile with her husband. She did not look as surprised as Melinda expected. "I'd be happy for you to do the cooking. It'll be a treat for me since I'll be busy baking bread tomorrow for the Missionary Society. You should still have time to go to town with Pa to get supplies. I've been wanting you to pick out material for new dresses for you and Annie. And Daniel needs a new shirt."

Melinda bit her lip. She hated going to town. She always felt like people were staring at her.

"I could do the baking while you go to town."

Rebecca shook her head. "It's good for you to take charge of things. You're almost grown now. Pa says we shelter you too much and I think he might be right. You have to face life. You can't hide."

Melinda remembered the painful episode when she was a young girl that had taught her that she was no more accepted by adults than she was by their children. She had been assigned to amuse her brother, Daniel, while the ladies sat in the kitchen having a quilting party for the Lewis girl who was about to be married. She had felt left out and decided to hover outside the kitchen door to listen. She had never forgotten what she had heard.

Mrs. Anderson had leaned toward Rebecca and said, "I'm not saying you shouldn't have taken the child. She's turning out rather well considering her background."

She paused to gesture toward the fair-haired baby sleeping in the cradle. "But how will she feel when your little Annie turns into a beauty and all the boys come courting her? You can't possibly believe any of the young men around here will want an Indian girl for a wife. She'll be all alone someday unless you return her to her own people."

An icy stillness settled on the group. Rebecca set down her square of quilting. Her mild manners were quick to be shed where Melinda was concerned. In a no-nonsense voice that Melinda recognized, Rebecca addressed Nellie Anderson. "Melinda is our daughter. We love her just as you love your daughter. Any young man who is not smart enough to see her beauty does not deserve her. I feel confident that someone will appreciate her worth."

Melinda had appreciated Rebecca's defense. But Rebecca could not always protect her. She had not been able to protect her from the cruel comments of the children at school. That was why she no longer attended school. Rebecca thought teaching her at home would protect her, that she would no longer have to hear hurtful remarks. But she was not safe from viperous tongues, even in her own home.

Her eyes had burned with tears. She had wanted to rush in and throw herself on her mother's lap as she had done that last dreadful day of school. Yet she dared not do so. They would all know she had been listening. And such ill manners might convince Mrs. Anderson that Melinda was as unlovable as she had implied.

That day had shown Melinda that time would not change her lack of acceptance by her neighbors. She had thought only the children scorned her, that when she grew up things would be different. But hearing the same ostracizing words from an adult had destroyed that hope. And it did something to her trust that could not easily be repaired.

Though she was a young woman now, she could still feel the sting of rejection. She had resolved to avoid those who caused it. Nevertheless, she knew it was no use arguing with Ma. She would have to grit her teeth and endure the trip to town. And she would have to ignore the way Mrs. Taylor, the shopkeeper, watched her as though she would have to clean everything Melinda touched.

They set out for town early the next morning. Melinda breathed deeply of the fresh scent of damp earth and the vanilla scent of ponderosa pines. The sky was bright blue and wildflowers lined the dusty wagon trail. She longed to spend the day in the mountain meadows. The daisies were in bloom and it was a perfect day for scouting wild berries or onions that would soon be ripe. Instead, she was headed to town with Joseph and the children.

Daniel drove the wagon with Joseph's help. Annie sat beside Melinda and begged, "Tell me about when I was born."

Melinda smiled at the golden-haired child and began the story she had told so many times.

"I came back from gathering eggs at the Bentley place and Pa told me to stay with Ma while he went for the doctor. I was awful scared because I didn't know anything about babies. I was at school when Daniel was born. I guess Daniel was worried too because he sat in the corner and sucked his thumb."

Annie laughed at the idea of her older brother sucking his thumb. "Tell more about me."

"I wiped Ma's face with a damp cloth and waited for Pa and the doctor. It seemed to take forever. When they came, I barely remembered the doctor. He had come out only once before when Daniel had been real sick with a stomachache."

Annie nodded thoughtfully.

"I made Daniel some supper and then I heard a baby crying. I ran into Ma's room and saw her holding you. She said we would call you Annie, after your grandmother. She let me hold you. You were so tiny. You had blond fuzz on your head and the softest cheeks."

She ran her finger along the child's face, noting that she was still smooth and baby soft.

Annie held up her doll. "Betty's soft too."

Melinda smiled down at the ragged calico doll with frayed hair, a doll only a tiny little mother could love.

Annie crooned to her baby as the wagon continued along its rutted route.

When they reached the store, Joseph helped his brood down from the wagon. "You stay with Melinda," he told Annie.

She nodded and clutched Melinda's hand. Joseph and Daniel were soon busy choosing grain and seeds for the garden. Melinda overheard Mr. Taylor tell Pa, "We're mighty concerned since we heard the rumor 'bout Fort Baxter being closed. Do you think it's true?"

Joseph rubbed his chin. "Could be. Since war's been declared between the North and South, they'll be needing the soldiers."

"Who's going to keep them Indians from coming back? You folks living out from town best hope the rumor's not true."

"Maybe the Indians have resettled and won't want to come back," Joseph replied.

Mr. Taylor shook his head. "I've heard there's unrest among 'em. God help us if they come here."

The conversation ended and Melinda became absorbed in the crisp fabric. Annie wandered with her among the prints, making suggestions about a dress for Betty to match her own.

Melinda stopped at a bright print. "Here, Annie, this is what you and Betty might like."

Annie pursed her cupid lips and said, "Betty likes it too."

When the fabrics had been chosen, Mrs. Taylor cut the needed yardage from the bolt. Then, taking Melinda's list, she filled their needs for dry goods. Joseph added his purchases and they waited together while the order was totaled.

The bell on the door jingled and they turned to see a woman enter. She was pale with dark hair and light blue eyes. A girl, who looked remarkably like her, followed at her elbow. They were laughing together, unaware of the party waiting at the counter. They came to an abrupt halt and stared at Melinda.

Mrs. Taylor broke the silence. "I don't expect you folks have met."

She nodded toward the newcomers. "This is Mrs. Abigail Newton and her daughter Elizabeth. They've come from Savannah to take over the running of the Talbot Hotel."

Abigail produced a formal smile and drawled, "Pleased to meet you, I'm sure."

She extended her hand to Joseph, who said, "I'm Joseph Pratt. It's good to know somebody's going to take over the hotel. I hated to see it close."

"It belonged to my Papa," said Mrs. Newton. "When he died, he left it to us. There was nothing to do but to come west and take over. I just hope Elizabeth can find a proper social circle for young ladies here."

Her eyes drifted back to Melinda. "Pardon my asking, but is this girl your Indian daughter?"

Joseph laid his hand on Melinda's shoulder. "Yes, this is Melinda."

"It was kind of you to take her in. The ladies in town told me how she came to live with you."

"Yes. There was a raid on her village when she was a tot."

Melinda lowered her eyes under Elizabeth's curious stare. She could imagine what the ladies in town had said.

Joseph turned to Mrs. Taylor. "Better figure what I owe you. I gotta be getting back."

"Of course."

She totaled the supplies and took his money.

He tipped his hat before hoisting the sack of grain. "I hope you ladies like it here."

"I'm sure we shall." Abigail smiled and Elizabeth gave a slight curtsey.

Melinda took Annie's hand and followed Joseph to the door.

She heard Elizabeth ask, "Does she sleep in the house with the family?"

"They treat her just like one of their own," Mrs. Taylor replied.

Melinda clenched her jaw in the habit she had formed in childhood to keep back tears of embarrassment. She lifted Annie into the wagon and climbed up beside her. Daniel helped Joseph load the dry goods before they climbed aboard.

While Annie played with her doll, Melinda sat in stiff silence, nursing her wound and wishing Joseph had never rescued her. She loved her family dearly, but would the rest of the town ever accept her? No one gave her the chance to show she only differed from them on the outside.

She paused in her thoughts. That wasn't entirely true. There was Will. He had always accepted her. Why couldn't the others be like him?

When they reached home, Joseph set Daniel to work unloading the wagon. He reached out to stop Melinda before she could follow Annie into the house. "Don't pay any mind to what that woman said. It was pure ignorance."

Melinda bit her lip. "I don't like being the town curiosity."

Joseph sighed. "It seems like you have two choices. You can let it break you and run away like a scared rabbit or you can hold up your head and face it."

He pointed toward the woods. "See that aspen over there?"

She nodded. She'd seen it many times.

"It got brittle and stiff last winter and broke apart. See the pine standing next to it. It bent with the wind and now it's standing tall and straight. Bend with the wind, Melinda. Don't let anybody break you."

"I'll try, but it's awfully hard."

"Of course it's hard. But it will make you stronger if you let it. Now, don't you have a supper to cook for a young man tonight?"

When he winked, Melinda flushed and turned toward the house.

She soon had the supper preparation well in hand. Chicken sizzled to golden crisp perfection and potatoes jostled in a frothing boil by the time Will rode into the yard.

She wiped her hands on her apron as Joseph greeted him at the door. "Haven't seen much of you in a while. They keeping you busy at the ranch?"

Will grinned. "Awful busy. We're expecting a bunch of new calves."

He set his hat atop the coat rack and grinned at Melinda.

"Sure smells good. Do you remember the last thing you fed me?"

She frowned, trying to remember when she'd cooked for him.

"It was mud pie," he said. "We must have been 'bout six years old. I can't believe I let you talk me into trying it."

She shrugged sheepishly, remembering how she'd convinced him it would taste good. "You should have known better."

He shook his head. "You could always talk me into anything."

Rebecca joined them, carrying a sleepy-eyed Annie who had just waked from her nap. "It's been nice having this break from cooking. Melinda's done everything."

Melinda felt her cheeks flush. "I better take supper up before it burns. Otherwise, Will might add that to the mud pie story."

Daniel settled next to Will at the table. "Pa says he'll get me a horse. He said maybe your pa would have one I could break come summer."

Will rubbed his chin, his dark eyes sparkling as he thought. "We're expecting two colts. I'll talk to Pa and see if he thinks we can spare one. I raised Ginger from a colt, you know."

"You did? Could you help me train mine?"

Joseph raised a hand, "Whoa. You can't go taking up Will's time. I can show you how to break a horse."

Melinda suppressed a chuckle. Daniel had always felt he'd been cheated out of having an older brother. He looked up to Will. Will, with his usual good nature, didn't seem to mind.

"Your pa knows all about horses. He was in the cavalry," Will reminded Daniel.

He nodded. "It don't matter who teaches me as long as I get a horse."

"Don't you think it's time we prayed so we can eat this supper?" Rebecca asked.

They bowed their heads and Joseph offered thanks for the bounty before them. When he finished, Will tasted the chicken and nodded his approval. "You can talk me into tasting this anytime."

Melinda smiled. "I've had some practice since mud pies."

"I'd say desserts are her specialty. I saw her putting together a chocolate cake when I came through the kitchen this afternoon," Rebecca said.

Will shook his head. "Poor Ginger. I'm gonna be so heavy, she won't like carrying me home."

At the mention of Ginger, Daniel launched into another barrage of questions about the expected colts.

"We don't know for sure if Will's pa wants to sell. Better not count your horses before they're born," Joseph said to quiet him.

He changed the subject by saying, "I heard your brother, Garrett's, taken up working at his father-in-law's ranch."

Will nodded. "Sybil's pa's in a bad way and can't do much anymore. The ranch is a real nice spread, but it needs a lot of work. He's taken on James and Peter as part-time hands when they can be spared from our place."

"If all your brothers go working other ranches, you're going to be the only one left at your spread," Melinda observed.

"Naw. James and Peter will never leave the ranch. It's in their blood. Can't say the same for me."

Their startled faces testified to their surprise. "What will you do if you don't stay on the ranch?" Melinda asked.

"I been thinking about going to Boston and studying medicine. I might come back when I become a doctor. Old Doc Baker won't be here forever and the town needs a doctor."

Rebecca nodded. "That's true. I don't know what I would have done without a doctor when Annie was born." She rubbed a finger along the child's soft cheek.

"But Boston is so far," Melinda stammered. "How long would you be away?"

"Could be four or five years until I finish and earn enough money to come home."

Melinda felt her appetite disappear. It was as if her only candle had blown out, leaving her to stumble into a dark future. What would she do while he was gone? What if he didn't return at all? She had always envisioned him as part of her life. She couldn't imagine the years stretching ahead with no hope of seeing him at church or riding across the meadow.

Loneliness settled like a stone in her chest. She did not relish living out her life alone. Most girls left their farms to get married. It occurred to her with sudden pain that Rebecca had been careful to teach her skills that would help her support herself. Perhaps Rebecca now agreed with Mrs. Anderson that Melinda would not find a man who would want an Indian girl for a wife. Perhaps they were right. No doubt Melinda could find an occupation, perhaps as a dressmaker, living all alone in a boardinghouse. That is, if she could find a boardinghouse that would take her.

"When are you thinking of leaving?" Joseph asked Will.

"Late next fall when we get past the chores. By then, James and Peter should be back full-time at the ranch."

Melinda had little to say during the rest of the meal. She forced herself to smile at the lavish compliments for her cake, yet was unmindful of the taste as she ate her slice.

When everyone finished, she began to gather the plates. Rebecca quickly intervened. "It's warm in here. You two go sit a spell on the porch and cool off."

When Daniel attempted to follow, Rebecca called him back with a command to fetch some water to wash the dishes. Reluctantly, he trudged off to the well. Annie helped her mother while Joseph occupied himself by feeding the livestock.

They sat together on the porch, not speaking until Will broke the silence. "Will you be sorry to see me go?"

She wondered if her face had given her away. Feeling transparent, she looked up in his eyes and saw an earnest need for an answer. She fumbled for words to express her thoughts. "I . . . I want you to do what will make you happy. I just didn't know you were thinking of leaving."

"I've thought about it for years . . . ever since Jesse died."

"But you were only a little boy then."

She remembered Will's little brother, who had caught pneumonia and died one winter when they were still quite young. It had taken a long time for Will to revert to a fun-loving playmate.

"I was about Daniel's age."

"You never said anything about being a doctor then."

"I didn't want to talk about it. It reminded me of Jesse's death. But all these years I've carried it around inside, feeling that's what I was intended to do."

She felt his eyes on her face as he asked, "How do you feel about it?"

"I wish you'd told me before. It came as a quite a shock."

His eyes showed concern when he asked, "What about you? What will you do while I'm gone?"

She shrugged. "Maybe I'll get a job in town soon. I can sew pretty well and I can cook." She nodded toward the remains of the meal.

"You might get married."

She fixed him with a level stare. "Do you remember when we were little and went to school? The looks I got and the unkind remarks? I still get them when I go to town. Maybe I'll be good enough to sew clothes, but who will want to marry me?"

She fought the bitterness that threatened to overwhelm her. Joseph said bitterness only led to unhappiness. Yet, sometimes it was hard not to be bitter.

"I always thought you were beautiful."

His honesty surprised her. She lowered her eyes, feeling her cheeks flush. "I'm afraid you were the only one who thought so."

"Didn't it help any that I was your friend?"

"It helped a great deal. You'll never know how much it meant to me."

"It meant a lot to me too." He looked at the stretch of land that separated their spreads. Dusk was descending. Crickets set up their night song.

"I enjoyed dinner, but I best be going."

The air was growing chilly. Melinda shivered as she rose from her chair. "I'll fetch your hat."

He called inside to bid the family good-bye while she retrieved his hat.

"I'm glad you came," she said.

He regarded her carefully. "I've been thinking about you lately and wondering if you changed much in the last few years."

"Have I?"

"Nope. You're still the smartest and prettiest girl around. I'll be busy at the ranch for the next few weeks, but I'd like to spend time with you before I leave."

"I'd like that too. Some of the berries should be getting ripe in a few weeks. We could go out picking."

"I'll look forward to it." He unhitched his horse and swung into the saddle. Her heart soared as she watched him ride across the meadow. Even though he planned to leave, he wanted to spend time with her.

She remembered the time when they were children and he had impetuously kissed her on the cheek. She had cherished that memory ever since. She touched her fingers to her cheek and thought that, perhaps, he would not forget her when he finished his schooling.

The next morning, Adam Smith came riding in from his spread to the west. He was a squat, terse man with a face weathered by the sun. He wore a scowl as he alighted.

Melinda paused in her butter churning and waited for him to state the nature of his business.

"Where's Joseph?" he asked.

"He's plowing the east meadow."

Rebecca joined Melinda on the porch. "Morning, Mr. Smith. Would you like to come in for a cool drink?"

"No thanks, ma'am. I gotta be warning folks to be on the lookout. The Davidsons' barn burned last night and the horses are missing. They think it was an Indian raid."

Rebecca caught her breath. "Oh my! Did they see them?"

"Nope. Didn't see a thing, just the fire."

"I'll tell Joseph when he comes in for lunch," Rebecca said.

Adam nodded. "I best be getting along. You folks keep a watchful eye."

Melinda turned to Rebecca. "Do you think it was an Indian raid?"

"I don't know. Could be. Without a strong fort, it'll be hard to keep order."

She smiled at Melinda. "I'm sure it's nothing to worry about."

Joseph wasn't so sure. When he came in for lunch, he said, "I've been wondering what would happen with so many soldiers called east. I been hearing rumors of trouble."

"I can shoot, Pa. I could sit up and guard the barn," Daniel offered.

Joseph ruffled his hair. "People are more important than barns, son. You'll sleep in the house like always. Maybe we'll get us a guard dog. I'll check with Thomas Bentley and see if he's got any dogs for sale. Will usually trains the hunting dogs for his pa. He does a fine job."

"A dog! Can I go with you to pick him out?" Daniel asked.

Joseph nodded.

"I could take him over this afternoon. I don't have any chores that need doing till supper time," Melinda offered.

"That would be a help," Joseph replied.

Rebecca shook her head. "I don't like the idea of them out alone. Not after what just happened at the Davidsons'."

Joseph rubbed the stubble of whiskers on his chin. His dark eyes were pensive. "They don't know for sure it was Indians. Even if it was, I expect Melinda and Daniel will be okay crossing the meadow. They'll be home long before dusk."

Melinda shivered, imagining shadowy figures lying in wait. She would have taken back her offer if it hadn't been for Daniel's expectant face.

"We'll come straight back," she promised.

Her fear subsided in the open meadow where the birds played tag above them and the sky lay bright and clear overhead. She drew a deep breath of the fragrant wild flowers. Surely there could never be danger in this glorious land between the ranches. She had ridden here often with Will and picked berries and columbines. Surely nothing would ever harm them here.

They reached the ranch house as the family was finishing the midday meal. "Hope we're not disturbing you," Melinda said when Mr. Bentley ushered them in. His strong chin and dark eyes reminded her of Will.

"Not at all. It's good to see you."

Will emerged from the kitchen. "If you'd come a little sooner, we could have repaid you for the meal I just ate at your place."

She smiled. "I didn't come to eat. We came to see if you had any extra pups around the ranch." Her face grew serious as she added, "We just heard the Davidsons' barn burned last night. Adam Smith said it might be Indians."

She stumbled over the last sentence and felt a self-conscious heat rise in her cheeks. The Indians were as far removed from her experience as they were the Bentleys, yet, they were as close as the blood that flowed through her veins. Speaking of them made her feel uncomfortable.

Mr. Bentley seemed unaware of her discomfort. He rubbed his hand across his lower jaw. "We haven't had any trouble, but that sure is worrisome news. I can see why you want a dog. We have a mongrel that sleeps in the barn. She had a couple of pups a while back. Maybe you'd like one of them. Will can take you to look at 'em."

"Pa said I could do the choosing, remember?" Daniel reminded.

She nodded. "I remember."

"I'm going to take care of the puppy and train it," he informed Mr. Bentley.

The older man bent to talk to Daniel. "Then you know it's a big responsibility caring for a dog. It's more than just playing with him and forgetting him when you're done. But since your gettin' to be grown, you should be able to take on the job."

Daniel beamed with pride.

"Come on. I'll show you the pups," Will offered.

They followed him to the barn, which smelled of horses, tackle, and grain. He whistled and a brown dog appeared, knee-high and wiry with broad shoulders. Two half-grown pups flanked her.

"We call her Sheiba. We haven't named the pups," Will said.

Daniel squatted and called to them. Sheiba growled a

low warning. "I'll shut her in the barn so you can choose from the two in this litter," Will said.

With Sheiba shut away, the puppies quickly warmed to Daniel. One tugged playfully at his shoe, licking his fingers when he pushed it away. "I want this one. I'm going to name him Rascal."

Will laughed. "Good name."

"We want to pay you something for him," Melinda said.

He shook his head. "We got enough dogs. This one would only be in the way. I'll fetch a rope and you can lead him home."

Melinda watched Will lasso the pup. He caught her staring at him and she blushed, wondering if he had any idea how handsome she found him. She walked beside him as he escorted them to the edge of the meadow that separated his ranch from her farm. They lingered a moment to say good-bye before starting home. Melinda looked back and grinned when she caught Will watching her. She gave him a parting smile, wishing she could have stayed longer. But she knew Will had work to do.

Rascal had his own ideas about where he would like to explore as they led him across the meadow. They arrived, at last, out of breath and laughing.

When Joseph came in for supper, he studied the dog. "I think you can make something of him, but it's gonna take some work."

"Can he sleep with me?" Daniel asked.

Rebecca rolled her eyes and Joseph chuckled. "He can sleep on the floor in your room until he gets used to staying here," Joseph said.

As Rascal adjusted to his new home, the family found

their patience tested. As soon as they arose, the puppy was underfoot, sniffing eagerly at the smells of bacon and biscuits. Melinda was always glad for the temporary relief from his eager presence when he followed Daniel to the fields each day after breakfast.

He became attached to Daniel and stayed dutifully within earshot when his young master was home. One day, however, Daniel left him on the porch while he and Joseph went into town. Later that morning, Melinda went out to churn butter. Rascal was nowhere to be found. Calling his name brought no response. She was beginning to wonder what had become of him when Will arrived with Rascal in tow.

He tied Rascal to the porch rail. Then he grinned at Melinda and said, "Guess he decided to pay a visit to his ma."

She apologized for the inconvenience and said, "He probably tried to follow the wagon to town, got tired, and decided to stop at your place. Thanks for bringing him back. He won't wander once Daniel gets home."

"I didn't mind. It gave me an excuse to come over."

She hesitated a moment and then decided that if he could be honest, so could she. "I always felt the same way about bringing jam to your place."

He studied her closely. "Did you? I guess you enjoyed those talks with Ma."

"I did. But I always hoped you'd come home while I was there. I missed seeing you after I left school."

"I missed you too," he said softly.

She flushed with pleasure at his confession. Then, realizing she was forgetting her manners, she said, "Would you like to come in for some coffee? We've got some already made."

"I wish I could, but I best be getting back."

She called to him as he turned. "I'm going berry picking on Saturday. Would you like to come?"

He tipped back his hat and regarded her with interest. "I'd like that a lot."

"Then I'll see you Saturday."

Her heart felt light as she finished the butter. Then she turned to the task of collecting the braided rugs for their weekly beating. Annie joined her, enthusiastically wielding a broom that Joseph had cut to her size.

Melinda could hardly wait for the rest of the week to pass. When Saturday finally arrived, she pulled her hair into a sleek chignon and slipped on a calico dress. Though faded, it was still a favorite because of the way it accentuated the slender curve of her waist.

Her anticipation grew as she waited for Will. Ever since he had come to dinner, he had seemed to regard her with special attentiveness, as though they had stepped past their awkwardness to explore what they had now become.

As she waited on the porch, Joseph spotted her and trudged over from the barn. "What are you aiming to do with that bucket?"

"I'm going berry picking."

A frown spread across his weathered face. His brows puckered with concern. "Crossing the meadow is one thing, but I don't like the idea of you going into the woods alone. We ain't heard of any trouble since the barn burning but that don't mean it ain't out there."

She glanced up to see Will riding toward them. A warm flush touched her cheeks. "I'm not going alone."

Joseph smiled as she turned a pleading face. "You be back before dinner."

"We will."

Will reined Ginger and slid from the saddle. He grinned as he held up his pail. "Hope they're ripe. I got out of fence mending by promising to fill this bucket."

"I'll have Daniel see to Ginger while you're gone. He'll think it's a treat," Joseph said. He pointed toward the woods. "Keep a sharp watch out there."

Will nodded. "That's what Pa said. I'll keep my eyes open. Also, we won't go beyond the creek." He motioned to the line of trees that edged a shallow stream.

Joseph led the horse to the corral while they set off for the creek.

Melinda cast a shy glance at Will. "I hope the berries are ripe. I'd hate to pull you away from work for nothing."

He grinned impishly. "But if they're not ripe, that would give me an excuse to go again."

Her pulse quickened with the growing assurance that it was she and not the berries that drew him to this task. She took a deep breath and said, "I hope you'll write me when you go east. I want to know how you like it."

He paused, studying her face as though he would memorize each detail. "I'll write until you get sick of hearing from me if you promise to write back."

"I promise. I hope you don't get bored with my simple letters. After all, you'll be in a big city with lots of excitement." She smiled to lighten the insecurity behind her words, yet she could not deny the worry that he would forget her.

He fixed on her with an expression she could not read, as though he yearned to say or do something, yet was not sure he should. "I'll be in a big city and I'll be lonely. I'll miss everything about this place. I'll miss berry picking and I'll miss seeing you come across the meadow with your jam."

She laughed. "When you see ladies in their fine clothes are you going to remember me carrying over a batch of jam?"

"No matter how fine they dress, they won't look any prettier than you do right now. I could never forget you, ever. I promise." He leaned over and kissed her gently on the cheek.

"You did that once before," she said. "I've always remembered it."

"Did I? When?"

"We were just children."

He studied her as he brushed back a strand of her hair that had pulled loose in the gentle breeze. "We're not children anymore. But I still like you just as much as I did then. And I still think you're beautiful."

Though Ma had told her often that she was pretty, the fact that she was different had kept her from believing it.

She smiled up at him. "If anyone could make me feel pretty, it would be you."

Approval shone in his eyes. He took her hand impulsively as he had often done when they were children. She enjoyed the feel of his sturdy, work-hardened fingers. She belonged with him. She always had. Yet, now, unlike their childhood days, she longed to be more than a pleasant companion. She had begun to hope he felt the same.

As they reached the edge of the trees, she remembered Joseph's warning to avoid being seen by Indians. It was not the first time he had warned her. Joseph had told her that if her people knew she was with them, they might come for her and take her away. When she was a small child, she had sometimes lain awake from the worry of being stolen from her bed in the night. Now, the rumors of raiding parties in the area produced a shiver down her spine as she experienced a reunion with her childhood fear.

They descended the embankment, hearing the song of the creek as it tumbled over the rocks, issuing a peaceful rushing sound. Squirrels ran between the trees, chattering from their perches as they watched the newcomers set to work on the ripe berries.

Melinda avoided the thorns with her nimble fingers and soon collected nearly a bucket of ripe fruit. She paused often to scan for shadows between the trees and was relieved when she had filled her pail. A glance at Will's half-empty bucket told her he had spent more time on lookout than he had collecting berries.

She suppressed a chuckle at his look of chagrin.

"I suppose you're all done," he said.

"Yes, I am." She smiled, pleased he had taken his promise seriously to keep a lookout.

Without a word, he tipped half her bucket into his and announced. "Now I'm done."

He baited her with a mischievous grin.

Her lips parted in surprise. "Why, Will Bentley!"

She laughed as he faced her, a figure of unrepentance. She cast about for a clever chastisement, but her rebuke was forgotten as foliage rustled on the opposite bank. Will motioned her behind a rock. They squatted, barely daring to breathe as they waited to see who would emerge.

Chapter Three

Melinda clutched Will's arm. She hardly dared breathe as she watched shadowy forms move among the trees. Her heart pounded as her vivid imagination conjured a raiding party in full war paint. Such was her relief that she nearly laughed aloud when a mother black bear and two cubs blundered out of the foliage. She let out the breath she'd been holding and felt her taut nerves relax. Beside her, she heard Will do the same.

When the mother bear took her cubs downstream, he said, "Guess we can get our buckets now."

She nodded. "I'm surprised they didn't eat our berries. I would have thought that was a small price to pay after what I imagined."

He rubbed his arm where she had squeezed. "I'm glad it was only bears or I wouldn't be able to use this arm."

She swallowed hard. Her heart still thumped from the scare. "You must think I'm a coward."

"I was behind the rock too."

She smiled at him, appreciating his kindness.

He picked up the buckets. "We should be gettin' back, though. We have enough berries."

They hiked back to the open meadow. The sun felt warm on Melinda's face as it thawed the icy dread that had filled her veins. They were safe. Everything was as it should be. The sky stretched in an endless blue canopy. Meadow hay grew tall in the fields as it did at this time every year.

These familiar surroundings gave her a sense of security. She could understand why Will had said he would miss them. She could hardly imagine leaving the only home she had ever known for a new life in the East. Her comfortable thoughts evaporated when she saw Rebecca hurrying toward them. She held a shotgun in her hands. Behind her, Annie stood on the porch, clinging to Daniel and sobbing.

Unaware of anything but Rebecca's anxious face, Melinda rushed forward. "What happened? What's wrong?"

"I'm so thankful you're back. I was worried sick. The old man who ranches next to us rode over with a bullet wound in his shoulder. Indians raided his place just before daybreak. Pa took him into town to see the Doc."

Relieved that nothing bad had happened to Pa, Melinda focused her attention on their neighbor.

"You mean the old hermit, Adam Smith?"

"Yes.

"Was he badly hurt?"

"He was pretty weak when he got here, but I think he'll live."

Will set the buckets on the porch. "Did they get his horses?"

"No. He managed to hold them off. He thinks he may have wounded one or two before he was shot."

Will rubbed his chin. "He'll need someone to look after things until he gets back. I can bring his horses over to our spread."

Melinda turned to him. "You're not going out there are you?"

"So far, the raids have all been before dawn. It should be safe to take a couple of ranch hands and go this afternoon."

Melinda shook her head. "It's not safe." She couldn't shake the fear that he might go and never return.

He placed his finger under her chin and gently lifted her face. "We'll be fine. It's you I'm worried about. First the Davidsons, then Adam. Your place could be next. Maybe I should sit on your porch for a few nights and keep watch."

She shivered. "And get shot? I wouldn't be able to sleep knowing you were out there in the dark."

He nodded reluctantly. "Then promise you'll be careful and stay close to the house."

Melinda remembered her scare down at the creek. "That's an easy promise."

He left her with a quick kiss on the cheek behind Rebecca's back and a warm feeling in her heart.

Joseph returned late that afternoon to a dinner they had kept warmed. "Adam's gonna be okay. Doc says it'll take a few weeks before he can use that right arm."

Rebecca ladled out stew. "Poor old man. Will said he'd care for the horses till Adam gets able."

Joseph nodded. "Ain't much else needs doing. The cows can graze. I can bring over the chickens to keep safe. He won't need the eggs as long as he's at the boarding-house where Doc can keep an eye on him."

Rebecca nodded. "We can use more eggs."

When he finished lunch, Joseph took Daniel out to join Will and the ranch hands in rounding up the hens and horses.

Melinda breathed a sigh of relief when they returned safely with two crates of noisy fowl. Annie made a great fuss over the hens, even giving them new names as they settled into the henhouse.

"They're not ours to keep," Rebecca reminded her. "They're just here until Mr. Smith gets well."

When dusk fell, the farm teamed with the usual sounds of night. Crickets sang and a soft breeze rustled through the old willow beside the porch. Instead of being com-forted by the familiar sounds, Melinda felt anxious lest these innocent noises mask the rustle of creeping invaders. She stared out the kitchen window. They could be out there, somewhere. They were Indians. Her people, yet foreign to her.

When she finally slid into bed, she lay awake, listening. Surely, Rascal would warn them from his tethered guard post on the porch. Daniel paused at her doorway on his way to his bed in the loft. He asked softly, "You think they'll come here?"

"What for? We only have two old horses, a few chick-ens, and two milk cows." She tried to sound reassuring.

"I think they might come anyway. Mr. Smith didn't have much and they went there."

Melinda shivered, wishing he would hush, yet knowing

he needed to talk. "Mr. Smith lives farther from town. So do the Davidsons. We'll be safe."

Their conversation ended as he climbed the ladder to bed. Melinda lay tense until exhaustion overtook her. She arose on Sunday, happy to be alive. Everyone in the family was eager for the outing to church.

After the service, everyone gathered in clusters to talk. Melinda stood with Rebecca, listening to Will's ma, Hannah Bentley. "Will said we ought to organize lookouts to keep watch for each other at night. He's worried about your place and would like to send some of our ranch hands over. Problem is, his brother Garrett needs our men on his ranch. With Sybil's pa ailing, Garret's the only able-bodied man on his ranch."

Rebecca nodded. "That's understandable. I heard Sybil's expecting."

Hannah beamed. "It's true. Can you believe it? Me, a granny."

"You'll be a wonderful granny."

Melinda studied Will as he leaned against a gnarled juniper talking to one of the ranchers. She wondered if he was excited about the upcoming new arrival. Did he want a family of his own some day? Did he think of her as a possible mate?

She had never been able to imagine a life without Will. Will had always taken care of her. He had always been her friend. She had spent her girlhood with the thought that they would be together forever, living comfortably on his ranch. When he had revealed his desire to travel east, it had severely shaken her girlhood dream. Could she adjust to the East if he asked her to join him? She bit her lip, thinking, and knew the answer lay in her heart. She would follow him anywhere in order to be his wife.

She shook herself out of her reverie and reminded herself he had made no commitment. He would soon be far away. Anything could happen between now and the time he returned from Boston.

She glanced up to hear Rebecca ask Hannah, "Who's that young man talking to Pastor Trent? Is he Elizabeth's beau?"

Melinda had seen the darkly handsome young man sitting with Abigail and Elizabeth.

"That's Abigail's nephew. He's come to help her run the hotel. Handsome thing, isn't he?"

"Why, Hannah Bentley! Shame on you for noticing." Rebecca delivered her chastisement with a grin.

Hannah laughed heartily. "I may be getting old, but I'm not blind."

Melinda studied the newcomer. His gray slacks and tailored coat were carefully cut to fit his trim form. His coat lay casually open to reveal a neat vest and a pale linen shirt. He presented a contrast to the farmers and ranchers whose Sunday best could not compare to such finery.

When he glanced her direction, she lowered her eyes and wished she'd been included in the grapevine of gossip exchanged by the other young women. Except for an occasional polite nod required in passing, they rarely acknowledged her, thus keeping her in the dark where news about newcomers was concerned. And she had no doubt that he'd been the topic of conversation since he arrived.

She looked up again as he bid the pastor good day, and then headed straight toward her. He caught her eye and she knew she was trapped. Though her instinct told her to flee from his obvious sophistication, it would be awkward to turn and bolt. She wondered what she would say if he spoke to her. She summoned her confidence with the knowledge that her manners were adequate, if not polished.

He tipped his hat and smiled. His teeth were even and white. "I'm Parker Newton."

He nodded to Hannah. "I believe we met in town."

She smiled in return. "Yes. I remember, but I don't believe you've met these ladies. This is Rebecca Pratt and her daughter Melinda."

"I'm pleased to meet you. Mrs. Bentley told me that your family makes the best jam around."

Rebecca laughed. "I don't know about that, but I'm pleased at the compliment."

"I would like to do more than offer a compliment. I'd like to offer a business arrangement. Neither my aunt nor cousin is inclined to take a personal hand in upgrading the cooking at the hotel. And it could stand improvement. As a first step, I'd like to buy your jams."

Rebecca shook her head. "I'm afraid we may not have any extra this year. Melinda picks the berries, but with the threat from Indians . . ."

"You don't feel safe in the woods." He fixed his eyes on Melinda. "That's understandable. What if I was to provide the berries? You could keep some for your own use and I'd buy jam you make with the rest."

Melinda flushed under his scrutiny.

"I think we should warn you the woods aren't safe for you either, Mr. Newton," Rebecca cautioned.

"Call me Parker. I won't have to go far and I'll be careful. I would pay you five cents a jar and I'll provide the jars. Do we have a deal?"

Melinda glanced at Rebecca, whose brow puckered thoughtfully.

"That's very generous of you. I don't have the time, but perhaps Melinda would like to consider your offer."

Melinda mentally added the income from the jars she could produce. It seemed a small fortune. Melinda had no doubt that Ma would help her make time to make the jam. Besides that, she knew Ma wanted her to have a source of income.

"I'll do it," Melinda answered, having every intention of sharing the profit with her family.

Rebecca regarded Parker for a moment, and then said, "Then it's settled. You bring the berries and Melinda will make the jam."

"Good. I'm glad that's arranged. I intend to offer the best food in the West. Your jams will be a first step in that direction."

He looked genuinely relieved as he added, "I better get back to the hotel. We'll have the noon crowd arriving for dinner soon. I'll bring jars and berries at the end of the week, if that would be suitable to you."

Melinda nodded, intrigued by the soft Southern accent. It fit his bearing as a Southern gentleman. His handsome lean face, sculpted chin, high cheekbones, and regal bearing gave him the appearance of aristocracy.

He tipped his hat and bid them good day, revealing carefully combed hair.

"Ambitious young man, isn't he?" Hannah observed when he had departed. She patted Melinda's arm and Melinda realized she had been staring after him. She couldn't put her finger on it, but something about him discomfited her.

"Now you'll be a woman of business," Hannah added.

Rebecca smiled at Melinda. "Sounds like he wants a lot of jam. I hope you know what you're getting into."

"I can do the work. But I'll feel terrible if harm comes to him while he's picking the berries."

"He did promise to be careful," said Hannah.

They watched him stroll to his buggy. Elizabeth joined her cousin after flashing a parting smile at Will. Will waved in return. His friendliness toward the newcomer gave Melinda a twinge of distress. She had always imagined that she occupied a monopoly on his attention where women were concerned.

She chastised herself for such naïveté. Though he lacked Parker's sophistication, Will possessed a pleasing personality and rugged good looks. When he was in town, girls probably flirted with him often. The thought that he might enjoy such attention was new to her and not a pleasant idea.

She tried to remind herself that she had no real claim on Will and must not count so strongly on his attention. To distract herself, she examined her impression of Parker. He was different from any man she had ever met. She wondered if he'd left a life of ease when he came to the untamed West.

Judging from their stylish dress, she would guess Parker, Abigail, and Elizabeth had all known luxury. She wondered what it would be like to wear fashionable frocks such as the ones Elizabeth wore. She imagined herself, dressed in velvet, holding Will's arm as she walked into church. Envy would be etched on to the face of every girl who saw her.

She shook her head, disgusted by her silly imagination. Such nonsense could only be a childish attempt to assuage her hurt feelings. Still, she admitted to herself that she eagerly anticipated her new position as a hired cook. She could only conclude that her feelings were the result of a lifelong desire to be acknowledged.

She sighed. Perhaps she'd been sheltered and lonely for too long if this bit of work made her feel worthwhile. Still, she welcomed the opportunity to have folks admire the fine jam and be told that it was made by Melinda Pratt.

After a restless Sunday afternoon that stretched into a restless night, she arose early to help Rebecca bring in eggs and start breakfast. When Annie arrived in the kitchen, sleepy-eyed and with her flaxen hair falling in a halo about her shoulders, Melinda set about the task of braiding her hair. She usually enjoyed taming her sister's soft tresses, but her wakefulness had left her in an irritable mood. Impatience assailed her. She bit her tongue to keep from scolding the squirming child while fastening the braids with ribbon that matched Annie's checkered dress.

"All done," she said with relief.

"Ma says we're going to the Bentleys' today. Daniel has to stay and help Pa in the fields."

Melinda paused in her daily ritual of twisting her own hair into a sleek bun. Holding a hairpin between her teeth, she asked, "Why are we going to the Bentleys'?"

Annie's incessant chatter was a habit the family had learned to tolerate with good-natured nods. Normally, Melinda paid it little heed. But her last remark had earned Melinda's full attention.

"I don't know. But you, Ma, and I are going. I'm glad

Daniel can't go. He gets to do more things than I do and it's not fair." Annie's lips puckered into a pout before she added, "I hope they have pie. They always have pie."

She was so cheered by the thought of a treat that she hugged Melinda around the waist. Melinda scooped her up and felt her ill humor disappear as Annie's arms closed around her neck. Annie was five now, and hardly a baby. Yet Melinda had a hard time accepting that Annie was growing up. Melinda cherished the years she had carried her around, feeling the soft hair against her cheek. Soon she would be too big to carry and her babyhood would be a thing of the past. She deposited Annie at the breakfast table just as Rebecca dished oatmeal into their bowls.

"You look tired, Melinda."

"I couldn't get to sleep last night."

Rebecca turned with a smile. "Maybe you're excited about your new employment."

Melinda had a more immediate claim on her attention. "Annie told me we're going to the Bentleys'."

Rebecca washed the oatmeal pan and placed it on its hook. Then she turned to face Melinda. "The missionary society is meeting at Hannah's house to knit hats and mittens. Since the war started, there's no telling how many women and children have been left in need. It's time some of you young women joined in the effort."

Melinda's interest ebbed to displeasure. "Who will be there?"

"Nellie Anderson is bringing her daughter, Becky, and Clara Baker will bring Susan. I don't know about the others."

Melinda didn't look forward to spending time with these young women. Becky Anderson was a flirt who showed no evidence of having a brain under her dark curls. Susan Baker had often been catty when they were in school.

Rebecca seemed to read her thoughts. "I know you don't feel comfortable, but that's all the more reason for you to go. You live in this town and you shouldn't have to hide. Besides, we can't think only of ourselves when the comfort of others is at stake."

Melinda couldn't deny her reaction had been selfish. Perhaps she could ignore any slights she might receive and take comfort in the fact that she rarely saw these women.

After breakfast, they climbed into the wagon and set off for the Bentley ranch. A carriage, parked in the yard, told her the ladies from town had arrived. Hannah greeted them warmly and brought them to the parlor. Melinda was surprised to see that Abigail and Elizabeth Newton had joined the rest of the group.

After everyone exchanged pleasantries, Hannah turned to Annie, "Would you like to take a slice of blackberry pie and a cup of milk to the back porch? There's a basket of kittens to play with when you're done."

Annie's face lit with delight. "Yes, please!"

Melinda wished she could escape so easily. Instead, she endured her position in the ring of chairs that had been brought in to form a cozy circle with the settee. In the center of the circle, a polished oak table held a tea tray and a plump blackberry pie.

Hannah nodded toward the pie. "Help yourselves, while I settle Annie on the porch."

Though Melinda had no appetite, she accepted a slice

of pie to occupy her attention. She nibbled at the crust and listened to the chatter of the other young women.

Clara poured the tea. She handed Rebecca a cup and said, "I worry about you folks outside of town. These are unsettled times and after what happened to poor Adam Smith . . ." She let the words trail off ominously.

Susan shivered. "I can't imagine living where I might be savaged in my sleep. I think I would rather die than live outside of town."

Elizabeth placed her empty plate on the table. "I'm sure I would die of fright before I could fire a single shot."

She turned to Melinda. "Aren't you just terrified . . . ?" She broke off and caught her lip between her teeth, studying Melinda as though she were seeing her for the first time.

Melinda glanced away. She set her half-eaten pie on the table and reached for her cup of tea. She felt it wobble and knew if she spilled it, she would run home and never return.

"Maybe they wouldn't hurt you since you're one of them," Elizabeth continued.

The room was quiet except for the ticking of the mantel clock. The women absorbed themselves with their tea. Out of deference to Rebecca, the older women had learned to avoid comments about Melinda. Elizabeth possessed no such sensibility. And now she was waiting for a reply.

Melinda imagined Rebecca had heard the comment. But Rebecca turned to speak with Mrs. Baker and Melinda knew she would not come to her rescue. Like a bird that had matured in the nest, Rebecca wanted her to learn to fly.

She took a sip of tea, and then said softly. "I don't know what they would do. I'm just as fearful as you are."

Hannah breezed back in the room, her ignorance of the tension as refreshing as a breath of fresh air. "Has everyone had pie? I hope so, 'cause my boys eat everything before I get a chance to serve it. I had to threaten to stop cooking to save this pie."

She plunked into a chair and picked up her yarn. "What's everyone planning to make?"

Abigail puckered her smooth brow. "I'm attempting to fashion a scarf. I haven't knitted one since I was a girl, but I'm sure I can remember how."

"I'm going to make mittens for the children. It seems they suffer most during a war," Rebecca said.

"I can't imagine why the North started this war. If they kept their noses out of our business, it wouldn't be happening at all," Abigail said.

"Did you have slaves?" Rebecca asked.

"Only two. My late husband was a merchant and we owned a house in town. But if I owned twenty, I would be sorely displeased with those who wished to release them with no compensation. Good slaves do not come cheaply."

"You have no problem with the buying and selling of human beings?" Rebecca's voice was mild, but Melinda knew there was strong conviction behind her question.

Abigail shook her head. Her eyelashes fluttered with impatience. "You people know nothing about it. Life is quite different here in the West."

"Yes. It is different, but people are the same. How would you feel if the Indians came and took you captive? You would be their slave. Would you consider that a fair arrangement for all the trouble they had gone to acquire you, or would you wish with all your heart to be free?"

There was a gasp from the women and open-mouthed surprise.

"Why, Rebecca Pratt, you can't mean to compare how Abigail treated her slaves to how she would be treated," Nellie protested.

"I simply mean to compare the situation of slavery. One group of people is not any happier to be made slaves than another whether they are Indian, black, or white."

Abigail's hands fluttered into her lap. For once she seemed at a loss for words.

Hannah broke the tension. "There's nothing we can do about our differences of opinion, but there is something we can do for those who will suffer. Let's pick up our needles and knit."

The women nodded and the group became less pensive.

"Are you entering a blackberry pie in the church fair?" Clara asked.

Hannah smiled. "Of course."

"I suppose there's no hope for the rest of us," Nellie said.

While the older women's conversation turned to talk of recipes for the fair, Elizabeth leaned conspiratorially toward the girls and whispered, "I'm glad Parker decided to come out here where he'll be safe from the war."

"Not half as glad as we are," Becky said with a giggle.

"I hear he hired you to make jam," Elizabeth commented to Melinda.

Melinda nodded. "As long as he's willing to bring the berries."

"He's a saint to try and do something about the food at that hotel before Mother and I starve. That grisly old man my uncle hired has cooked there for years. Neither Mother nor I will eat what he cooks. Parker is going to fire him and bring a cook from the South."

"When will the new cook come?" Susan asked.

"On the next stage."

Melinda had never eaten at the hotel. Still, she'd never heard anyone complain about the food until the Newtons arrived. Perhaps they were used to much finer fare than this town could offer.

At noon, they packed their knitting. Nellie collected the finished garments to store until there were enough to send east. As they were bidding their hostess thanks, Melinda saw Will striding toward the house.

As he approached the women, he tipped his hat. Elizabeth stepped out from the group. "Will Bentley. It's such a pleasure to see you. I haven't forgotten I promised you a dinner at the hotel. Don't you forget either."

Though Elizabeth seemed comfortable with such brashness, a flush crept into Will's cheeks. His grin was abashed. "I haven't forgotten."

She smiled and dimples showed on her cheek. "If the new cook hasn't come, I'll cook it for you myself."

Abigail leaned toward Will. "Take my advice and wait for the cook."

Elizabeth showed her dimples again. "Mother's right. I don't know a coffeepot from a skillet. But I do hope you'll come to dinner."

With a swish of her skirt she departed for the carriage, flanked by her companions. She was pretty. No wonder Will seemed taken with her. Her dark hair was netted carefully under in back and her eyes were so blue they rivaled the summer sky.

What did Melinda have to offer that would compete? She could cook a good meal. She had proved that. Yet, Elizabeth seemed to wear her lack of domesticity like a badge. Perhaps it wasn't an asset where she came from. And perhaps Will didn't mind.

The witless grin faded from his face as he turned to Melinda. "You haven't been picking any more berries, have you?" There was genuine concern in his eyes.

"No. I haven't. Parker Newton will be bringing me berries. He's asked me to make jam for the hotel." She was glad for the surprise on his face. She couldn't forget the way he had blushed for Elizabeth.

She flashed him a curt smile. "I'd better find Annie."

They collected the youngster and set off for home. Rebecca glanced at Melinda. "I hope you weren't upset by what Elizabeth said."

Years of resentment churned in her heart. "I don't belong here. But where do I belong?"

Rebecca sighed. "You belong where you are loved. And you're loved by everyone who matters."

As they rattled down the rutted lane, she continued, "The Good Book says we are to love our neighbors. It's easy to love a neighbor like Hannah. There's no credit in that. People like Abigail and Elizabeth are harder to love. Maybe you should pray for Abigail and Elizabeth."

Melinda clenched her lip between her teeth. She would pray all right. She would pray they would go back to where they had come from.

As for Parker Newton, she wasn't sure about him yet. Susan and Becky had obviously been taken with him. She would know more about him Friday when he brought the berries.

"Will you try to forgive them?"

Rebecca's voice pulled her from her thoughts. She felt guilty as she looked into the gentle face.

She nodded. "I'll try."

Rebecca patted her arm. "Wait till they taste what wonderful jam you make."

Melinda remembered Parker's dark eyes and commanding presence and found herself suddenly worrying about whether he would like her jam.

Chapter Four

The next day passed in a busy cycle of chores. After supper, Melinda went outside to take the dry clothes from the line strung between the willow and a sturdy little juniper. She inhaled the sharp scent of pine and the sweet scent of clover. She longed to stay outside where the breeze of early evening offered relief from the heat of the kitchen. However, the pile of stiff clothing that rested across her arm reminded her of the flat iron that was heating on the stove.

Just before she started inside, she saw a horseman riding toward her from the far pasture. She frowned, hoping he was not the bearer of bad news. Then, she recognized him and bit her lip. It was Will. The memory of how he had smiled at Elizabeth still hurt.

She set the clothes on the porch, smoothed her skirt and re-pinned a lock of hair that had strayed from her bun. Then she stood watching while he dismounted and walked Ginger the last hundred yards to help her cool down.

He called a greeting to Melinda as he tied the horse to the small juniper.

"If you're looking for Pa, he's in the house," she said.

Will shook his head. "It's you I came to see."

Her resolve to protect her heart dissolved. She clutched the clothes like a protective shield and replied, "You shouldn't ride so late. It's not safe."

He grinned. "Are you worried about me?"

She pursed her lips. "Of course. I'd be worried about anyone who hadn't the good sense to stay home at dusk."

"It's the only time I can get away. Pa keeps me busy during the day. He'll keep me busy till the day I leave for Boston."

"That should help the time pass faster."

"Too fast."

Her heart skipped a beat at his wistful tone. Her pulse began to dance as she looked into his eyes and saw a longing for her there.

"Do you have time to sit on the porch?" he asked.

She wavered. "I'm heating the iron, but I suppose it will keep a little longer."

She took the clothes into the house, and then returned to settle herself on the top step beside Will. They stared into the gathering darkness until Will broke the silence. "I've been having second thoughts about going East."

His announcement surprised her. After he'd held this dream close for so many years, she wondered why he would reconsider.

She stared at him. "Your plans are all made. Why would you change your mind?"

He studied his hands. They were broad and competent. She'd already begun to think of them as doctor's hands.

He didn't answer for a long time. Finally he said simply, "I'm scared."

"Scared? Of what?"

"Of coming back and finding things have changed while I was away."

She shook her head. "Things don't ever change here."

"But they might. I could be gone several years. I might come riding down this road and find out . . ." He paused, staring out across the pasture.

"Find out what?" she prodded.

He turned and looked at her. "Find out you got married and had three kids."

She looked back into the dusky night, her heart hopeful as she asked, "Who would marry me?"

He took her chin and gently turned her to face him. "Do you think you are unattractive? Have you looked in the mirror lately?"

Was he telling her he loved her? Asking her to wait for him? Her heart beat so hard she thought it would surely leave her chest. She lowered her eye to the familiar cleft in his chin. She longed for him to clarify his feelings. So she stated, "I look in the mirror every morning and I don't see anyone this town would admire the way they admire girls like Elizabeth."

He pondered a moment, his brows drawing into a frown. "You don't look anything alike, but, if you ask me, you're much prettier. Besides that, you have a sweet nature that everyone should admire."

He paused, seeming to struggle for more words. Just then, Daniel bounced out the door with Rascal. The dog greeted Will enthusiastically. The words he wanted to speak and the mood of closeness were lost in the commotion.

"Rascal sleeps out here to watch for Indians," Daniel said.

Will rubbed the dog's ears and was rewarded by a moist tongue.

"I've taught him to stay on the porch," Daniel added.

Will smiled at the boy. "You're letting him earn his keep. That's important for a dog. And a boy." He ruffled Daniel's hair. "Why don't you get Ginger for me?"

"Okay." He hurried out to untie the horse.

Will stared after him.

"It's getting dark. Be careful going back," Melinda said softly.

He ran his hand tenderly along her cheek. "I will. Would you mind if I came to see you again in a few days?"

His tentative tone touched her heart.

"No. I wouldn't mind. I like to see you."

Daniel returned with Ginger. "Your horses had any foals yet?" His dark eyes were hopeful.

"Nope. I'll let you know first thing when it happens," Will promised. He swung into the saddle and tipped his hat. Turning quickly, he headed home.

Melinda touched the spot on her chin where his warm fingers had touched her face. She felt certain now that he cared for her. Yet, in spite of his compliments, she worried about holding his affections when she competed with girls like Elizabeth.

When she went to bed that night, she turned to her favorite verses in the Song of Solomon: "I am dark, but comely, O ye daughters of Jerusalem, as the tents of Kedar, as the curtains of Solomon."

She was dark. Did Will find her as comely as Solomon

found this girl? If so, then her love for him, sealed within her heart, could bloom in the sunshine of his love.

She continued reading, getting to her favorite line, "Many waters cannot quench love neither can the floods drown it."

She finished the chapter and sighed. It was a romantic book and she was in the mood for romance. She closed her eyes, hoping to dream of Will. To her surprise, her thoughts were drawn to Parker. She had an image of his dashing figure swinging up into the buggy. She contrasted him with Will and realized that he lacked the openness that characterized Will.

She shook his image from her mind, deciding that he was new and exciting, a wickedly handsome man who would capture the town girls' imagination. But not hers. Her heart belonged to her childhood friend.

When Friday morning arrived she arose, anticipating the arrival of the berries to make her jam. She donned a clean summer dress and pulled her hair into a neat chignon. Parker was a Southern gentleman, used to refined women. She could not compete with gentility, but it seemed terribly important that he not think that he had hired an untidy farm girl.

She went from task to task in a nervous flutter, scolding herself for her obsession over a simple business arrangement. Still, she was unable to repress the concern that he would withdraw his offer. By late afternoon, she had begun to wonder if he was coming at all. Perhaps he had decided berry picking was too tedious and decided to call off the arrangement. A cloud of disappointment settled over her as she hoed the vegetable garden.

She had so thoroughly convinced herself of his change

of plans that she was surprised when his buggy made the turn into the lane that led to the farm. She brushed the dust from her skirt and smoothed her hair. He waved a greeting and she returned the wave, though she was dismayed that he would find her dirty from garden work. She took a deep breath as she watched him slow the team to a walk. Then, taking a deep breath, she left her hoe in the garden and walked out to meet him. She hoped her manners, at least, would suffice.

He drew the team to a halt and tipped his felt hat. "Good afternoon, Miss Pratt. I trust you're still interested in our agreement."

She nodded. "I am. Did you bring the berries?"

"And the jars." He patted the seat beside him.

"I'll help you get them to the house," she offered.

He shook his head. "I wouldn't think of it. The boxes are much too heavy. You can keep me company while I unload them."

He flashed an engaging smile, then lifted the boxed jars with an ease that proved that his stylish attire disguised a muscular frame.

He glanced at Melinda. As they walked toward the house, he admitted, "You intrigue me. I heard you were rescued from a massacre when you were very young. Do you remember anything about it?"

She shook her head. "No. Nothing at all."

"Was it hard, growing up the only Indian girl in town?"

"Sometimes, yes. I wasn't well accepted as a child. Mostly I was ignored."

A frown creased his smooth forehead. "What a pity. I'd think you would interest most people." He smiled and added, "You interest me."

At a loss for a reply, she said, "Tell me about the place you come from."

"Ahh, it's beautiful. Lots of fine houses and fields of cotton. I'm going back there sometime to build a fine new hotel. It will be the best the South has ever seen."

She smiled. "It sounds like a wonderful dream."

"Perhaps you will be a part of it. Can you make enough jam for two hotels?"

She glanced at him. Was he teasing? His expression suggested he was not.

"You think I could turn jam making into a business?"

"Sure. We could be partners someday. I like a woman with a head for business."

She felt a flush creep across her cheeks at the implied compliment and hastened to direct him up the porch steps and into the kitchen. Rebecca glanced up from stirring a pot of stew that sat atop the cast-iron stove. She and Parker exchanged greetings as he set the box gently onto the plank floor.

"With all these jars, you must have found a bushel of berries," Rebecca said.

He nodded. "Enough to keep Miss Pratt busy."

He carried back a crate of ripe berries from his next trip to the buggy. A quick glance told Melinda they would make at least eight jars of jam. There would be a nice profit after Parker took out his expenses.

"How soon do you want them?" she asked.

"Soon as possible. Monday, perhaps?"

"I can make them by then."

"Good. I'll see that they are picked up and that you are paid."

He nodded toward the pot that simmered on the stove.

"I can tell by the aroma in this kitchen that I've put my investment in good hands."

Rebecca raised her eyebrows, surprised by a compliment for something she took for granted. "Thank you, Mr. Newton. Would you like to stay for supper? Joseph and Daniel will be in from the field any moment."

He bowed gallantly. "I'd be delighted."

"Good." She turned to the little girl who peered bashfully from behind her skirt. "Annie, you set the table. Melinda can slice some bread and spread it with jam while I take up supper."

"What can I do to help?" Parker asked.

"You can sit right there at the table and tell us about yourself," Rebecca said.

"I would not want to bore you ladies."

"I'm sure we'd find it interesting," Melinda assured him.

"Very well." He took a seat at the table and sipped from the coffee Rebecca handed him. "My mother died when I was quite young and my father traveled a great deal. So, I spent a lot of time with my Aunt Abigail. Her husband was a shrewd businessman who owned a dry goods store. He encouraged me to do well in school with the plan that I would go into business too. I think he hoped I would take over the store one day."

"Why didn't you stay to run the store when your uncle died?" Melinda asked.

My grand uncle passed away right after my uncle died. He left my aunt this hotel. There were some debts to be paid on the store. So, my aunt sold it to pay off the debts and moved here. I was disappointed about the store at first. But when she offered me an interest in the hotel, I realized my new opportunity."

"The town will be glad you, your aunt, and cousin came. The town needs a good hotel." Melinda felt as though she were fibbing if she included herself. She was not the least glad that Elizabeth had come.

She set the bread on the table. Joseph and Daniel entered, fresh from washing up. Joseph extended a hand in greeting. "Now I know why I didn't recognize the buggy."

As expected, Daniel was taken by Parker's fine horses and asked about them.

"Bought them here in town," Parker said. "They are adequate, but not nearly as fine as horses raised in the South. Southern horses put those two to shame."

"Really?" Daniel asked.

As supper progressed, the conversation involving horses grew lively, with Parker graciously but steadfastly refusing to agree that Western horse breeding equaled that of the South.

"I'm getting a foal from the Bentleys. You should see their horses," Daniel said.

"I should like to do that. In fact, I would like to hear more about all your neighbors."

They chatted about the other homesteaders, people in town, crops, and horses. All the while, Melinda felt impatient to change the subject back to the other world called "the South." She had spent her entire life on this farm and was eager to experience, even secondhand, the extravagance and beauty that he had hinted existed in his former surroundings.

When Rebecca finished describing their church socials, Melinda took the opportunity to ask, "What did you do for fun before you came here?"

He smiled. "There were always dinners and parties and I spent time on my hobby."

"Which was?" she prompted.

"Fencing. I don't wish to be immodest, but I've become quite adept."

Daniel's brows drew into a puzzled frown. "Fencing? That's hard work. I've given Pa a hand when we've had to mend a section."

Parker laughed. "No. You don't understand. I mean sword fighting. It's a gentleman's sport."

Melinda remembered seeing pictures in a book of two men engaged in fencing. She flushed. She did not wish to admit she had been as ignorant, at first, as Daniel.

"Swords. How exciting. I'd like to see that sometime," Daniel said.

He laughed. "I would be delighted to demonstrate if I can find a challenger."

She tried to imagine Will in fencing attire. The picture made her want to laugh. He could rope a steer and shoot as straight as any man in town. But she was sure he would have no use for "gentlemanly sport."

When supper was over, Parker smiled congenially and said, "That was a delightful meal. I enjoyed the company and the jam met my best expectations. However, I had better get back before my aunt works herself into a nervous worry."

"We're glad you stopped in," Rebecca said.

Melinda got his hat and coat. "I'll begin on the jam tomorrow."

"I look forward to including it on our new menu."

He paused at the door and took her hand. He held it

gently between his own palms. "It was a pleasure, Miss Pratt."

She felt her cheeks grow warm. Only Will had ever held her hand with such friendly intimacy. She longed to snatch it away, but dared not do so without causing offense. Instead she said simply, "Please call me Melinda."

"Melinda. I shall look forward to our next meeting."

He bowed, released her hand at last, and stepped out the door. She closed it slowly, giving time for the blush to fade from her cheeks. She was glad there were dirty dishes to be washed. Perhaps that mundane activity would take her mind off the discomfort the physical contact with Mr. Parker had caused.

Later, as she stood in her bedroom thoughtfully brushing her hair, Daniel paused in the doorway to ask, "Do you like him?"

"Who?"

"Parker."

"I suppose I should. I have no real reason not to."

"Well, I don't like him."

Taken aback, she turned to look at the boy. "Why not?"

"He brags too much. I bet he can't ride near as well as Will."

"That doesn't mean you shouldn't like him."

"Well, I don't."

She shrugged, tamping down the impulse to agree with him as he headed for the ladder up to the loft. Parker did seem rather taken with himself. Yet she would put up with him for the opportunity he represented. He could offer her the chance to become a woman of importance. One day, she might own a bakery and supply jams and desserts to his hotels. The girls who had turned their backs on her would look on her with envy. With these pleasant thoughts brewing in her mind, she fell asleep.

She awoke early, eager to begin her chore. She started a fire in the stove and began to cook her berries. By the end of a long day in the warm kitchen, she had eight jars filled and sealed with wax.

After supper, she retreated to the porch to catch a cool breeze. She had not been there long until she saw Will riding rapidly toward the house. As soon as he slid from the saddle, she knew from his grave expression that this was not a social visit. Something was wrong.

"Garrett's ranch was raided last night. They took six horses and killed one of the ranch hands."

Melinda caught her breath. "Who was killed?"

"A new guy named Pete. He was on lookout at the corral."

"That's awful. Who did it?"

He shook his head. "We didn't see. We tracked six riders into the woods before we lost the trail. Could be Cheyenne."

The rest of the family came onto the porch and Will repeated his story. "Sounds like they're after horses. Doubt they'll bother us since we have only two old nags. Just to be safe we'll keep them in the barn at night, though," Joseph said.

Will stooped to talk to Daniel. "I know you were hoping for a colt, but my brother lost six horses. He's going to need those colts we're expecting."

Daniel's face showed his disappointment. "You won't have any to sell?"

"I'm sorry. Maybe next year."

Joseph put his hand on Daniel's shoulder. "He knows family comes first. You have an obligation to your brother's ranch."

Daniel bit his lip, yet managed to nod his understanding.

"How's Sybil?" Rebecca asked.

"She was pretty shook up. Garrett sent her over to stay with Ma until the baby comes."

Rebecca nodded. "She's safer there."

"Yes. But she worries a lot about Garrett."

"I pray for the day when this will be over and we'll be safe again," Rebecca said.

"These are unsettling times most everywhere in the country. I don't suppose there's much safety to be had," Joseph said.

After Will headed home, Melinda sat up a long time thinking about the war in the East and the danger right at their door. Was there peace anywhere? Rebecca always said the only peace you could count on was the peace in your own heart. Perhaps she was right.

The mood was sober at church that week. After the service, small groups gathered to discuss the newest raid. "Might get a posse together to take after these renegades," suggested one rancher.

Another shook his head. "Likely get ambushed. We're better off to lie in wait at the ranches."

There was a lively debate before they decided a posse would leave too many of the ranches shorthanded. Melinda noticed that Parker did not take part in the conversation. Instead, he stood beside her and listened. His silence didn't surprise her since he had no ranch with which to concern himself.

When the men disbursed, she turned to him and said, "I finished the jam."

"Did you?" He smiled down at her. 'I'll make sure it's picked up first thing in the morning. We can serve it with biscuits at noon."

"Will you be wanting more next week?"

"Yes. Perhaps we could offer a different kind for variety. You know the woods better than I do. What berry would you suggest?"

"Wild strawberry or maybe chokecherry. In the fall I could make blackberry."

He shook his head. "Chokecherry? That's a new one for me."

"They're sour on the bush, but make good jelly. I could show you some. They're just starting to get ripe."

He tipped his hat. "I might just take you up on that offer."

He glanced toward his buggy. "I see my cousin and aunt are waiting at the buggy, and the result of keeping Elizabeth waiting is not pleasant. For all her outward beauty, she can be a trial sometimes." He gave her a conspiratorial grin before joining his cousin.

She watched him climb up and swing his long legs into place. She was surprised to hear a voice beside her. She turned to see Will. "Looks like you have a new admirer."

He did not sound pleased.

Her cheeks flushed. She was sure it was not true. Nonetheless, she wondered briefly how it felt to have several men competing for her attention like some of the other girls. The thought faded quickly as she turned to Will.

"I assure you I have no interest in Mr. Newton. I'm

making jam for his hotel. I have to do something while you're away. And his business arrangement holds more possibility for me than I ever thought possible. He plans to open a fancy new hotel in the South someday. Supplying him with jam could help me become a business woman."

When Will grew taciturn, Melinda continued, "If my jam becomes popular, I might make it for other hotels. I could hire extra help and someday I might even open a bakery and make breads and cakes. It could provide an excellent living."

She paused, expecting some encouragement regarding her enterprise. She was hurt and puzzled when it was not forthcoming. Instead, he studied her as though she was someone he had not known all his life.

"Is there a problem with my plans?" she demanded at last.

"No. It's just not what I imagined for you. I'm afraid that dandy is putting ideas in your head. And I like you the way you are."

Her irritation grew. What did he expect from her? That she would sit around and wait, hoping he would come back and still want her?

"Well, *I* don't like me the way I am. I'm tired of being a nobody here. You plan to trot off to Boston and you expect everyone to be happy for you. Why is it different when I have a dream of my own?"

The set of his jaw and his guarded expression told her he was upset. "It's not. If that is your dream, I hope you get what you want."

"I have to do something, Will. I can't sit at home for years, writing you letters and letting the days slip by.

Parker has given me a chance to rise above what I've always been. And I appreciate that."

He tightened his lips to a thin line. "I never thought you needed to rise above what you've been."

Her patience exhausted, she shot back, "You've always been accepted. You don't know what it's like not to be, how difficult it's been for me."

"I do know. I was your friend a long time before Parker showed up and I never minded what anybody thought or said. I'm sorry you did." He turned and walked to the wagon where his family was gathered for the ride home.

In all the years they had been friends they had rarely had a spat. He was the one person she could count on to understand her feelings. Why was he being difficult now?

Tears welled in her eyes. She'd been happy about her new opportunity. It had been unkind of Will to make her feel bad, especially since she didn't understand why he objected.

She wiped away the tears with her finger and hoped her family would not notice her moist lashes when she joined them for the ride home.

She felt out of sorts and ill-humored all afternoon. When she spoke sharply to Annie for playing loudly with Rascal, Rebecca cast a questioning look.

Melinda sighed and said, "I'm sorry, Annie. I'm feeling tired today."

Annie's blond curls bobbed. Her wide blue eyes filled with childish wisdom. "You need a nap."

"Yes. I suppose I do. I think I'll lie down for a while."

"And I'll play real quiet so I don't wake you," Annie promised.

She smiled at the child. "I know you will."

Alone in the room, she lay across the bed to think. Why was Will uncomfortable with her plans? Was it Parker's influence he was worried about? He had said that he was afraid that she would change too much while he was gone. She intended to change, for the better, to become independent and resourceful. Surely that would make him proud of her.

Then a new thought struck her. Perhaps he worried she would no longer need him when she became a successful woman of business. Her irritation evaporated as she considered this possibility. Of course she needed him. She cared desperately what he thought of her. That was why her afternoon had been ruined when he expressed reservation about her new venture.

She would find a way to assure him that her feelings for him would never change. He had always been her best friend and nothing could change that fact, not Parker, or anyone else. Her thoughts shifted to Parker. He would come in the morning to pay her and collect the jam. Will was surely wrong in suggesting that Parker had any other interest in her. It was a business arrangement and nothing more.

The next day, she did her chores on the porch and in the garden so she wouldn't miss the sight of his buggy. But when she heard horses approaching, she was surprised to see a large black man driving a wagon up to the farm. Rebecca came out to stand beside her as he alighted and tipped his hat. He was bald except for tufts of silver hair that lay on each side of his head, showing that he was at least middle-aged.

"I've come to collect the jam and bring Miss Melinda her money." He looked questioningly at the two women.

"Oh . . . Parker must have sent you," Melinda said.

He grinned, showing an even row of white teeth. "I'm Eli. Mr. Parker brought me and my wife out to work at the hotel. I used to belong to Mr. Parker's uncle, but I'm gonna be free as soon as I pay Mr. Parker for the trip out here."

Melinda shivered. The concept of one human belonging to another made her uneasy. She was glad Eli would be free.

They showed him into the kitchen where the jam sat in a small crate. As he carried them to the wagon, Melinda asked, "Is Parker paying you for working at the hotel?"

"No, Miss. Least, not yet. Like I says, we got to pay off the trip. My wife Besse is cooking for the hotel and I'm helping with the chores. When we pay back Mr. Parker we're gonna save up some money and buy a farm."

"That would be nice."

Eli dug in his pocket and produced the money. He handed it to Melinda, and then turned back to the wagon. "Mr. Parker sent more jars and another bucket of berries. He says if you have time, he'd like another little batch of jam."

"When does he have time to do all this picking?" Rebecca asked.

Eli laughed. "Mr. Parker don't pick any berries. I pick the berries."

He carried the jars and buckets into the kitchen and tipped his hat. "I best be gettin' back. I'll pick up the jam and the buckets on Wednesday if you think you'll be done by then."

"I'll be done."

As Eli drove away, she stood on the porch and counted

the money. She'd made twenty jars of jam at five cents a jar. Taking out expenses, she would be able to keep most of the money. And she would be paid again on Wednesday.

She glanced up to see Rebecca watching her. "Honest work is nothing to be ashamed of and you deserve decent pay. But don't ever start to worship money. It makes a mighty poor god."

She felt her cheeks redden. "I won't. It's just I've never had so much before."

Rebecca smiled. "Then you should enjoy it for the moment. When you're ready, put it away and finish your chores."

Melinda followed Rebecca into the house and tucked the money into the top drawer of her pine dresser. Before she went to bed that night, she took it out again, enjoying the cool feel of the coins. They were security, security that no matter what happened or what anyone said about her, she could earn her own way.

The next day was exhausting as she struggled to keep up with fitting in the jam making with the other chores around the house. Only the thought of the money that would collect in her drawer made it worth the effort.

At twilight, she finished setting out the freshly washed dishcloths on the porch rail to dry, then sank onto the step to rest and take in the coolness of the evening. Rebecca finished drying the dishes and joined her, settling into the creaky old rocker. Soon Annie curled into her mother's lap.

"You look tired tonight," Rebecca told Melinda. "Making so much jam is a lot of work on top of your other chores."

Melinda nodded. "It will be worth it."

"I suppose it will. You've never minded working hard. Even when you were a little girl you took pride in doing a woman's work. Sometimes I'd look into your little face and worry that you were trying too hard to grow up. I liked it when Will came to play and you could be a little girl, having fun."

Rebecca gazed across the meadow that separated their lands and Melinda wondered if she were looking for him now. "He's always been good for you."

Melinda wasn't sure how to reply. He was the one who had chosen the separation that would put him in Boston. She wanted to accept the fact that he was going away, and then to be happy going on with her life. She just wasn't sure that she could.

She watched the oats swaying in the field and said, "It was fun to have those carefree days, but we're not those children anymore. It's time to think of the future."

Rebecca stroked Annie's golden hair. "And you should. Just don't ever take so much pride in being independent that you shut others out of your life."

It was as though Rebecca had read her thoughts and knew her needs. But if that was the direction her life took, was it really her fault? Hadn't she been forced into this position by the luck of the draw in being brought here?

Melinda opened her mouth to protest. Yet, her words remained unspoken as she spotted a figure moving among the trees that lined the creek bank. The dwindling light made it impossible to tell if it were man or animal.

"What is it?" Rebecca asked.

She squinted and saw more movement. It had not been her imagination. Melinda's eyes were sharp but the descending twilight was working against her. Nonetheless, something was creeping through the field, moving toward the house.

She pointed. "There's something out there."

Rebecca rose and carried Annie to the house. Melinda was close behind.

"Pa and Daniel are in the barn. They won't have any warning if there's trouble. Fetch the rifle, and then stay in the house with Annie."

Melinda did as Rebecca bid. She handed Rebecca the gun and asked, "What are you going to do?"

"I'm going to fire a warning shot and pray it's coyotes I'm scaring off and not a raiding party planning to surprise us."

Her voice was shaky, yet her aim was steady as she pointed the rifle into the field. Melinda held Annie close as they watched from the window.

Chapter Five

Ma's shot rang out. It resounded for miles in the clear mountain air, stilling the night sounds of birds and crickets. Melinda cracked the door so that she could see the field of oats. Though she watched closely, she saw no hint of movement. Time seemed to stand still until Rascal set up a fierce barking from the barn. Joseph and Daniel appeared in the doorway. They peered out to see Rebecca pointing the shotgun into the field.

Crouching low, they raced to the porch with Rascal on their heels. Rebecca handed the rifle over to Joseph and said, "Melinda said she saw something creeping through the oats. I'll feel real silly if I'm shooting and yelling to scare off some jackrabbits."

They retreated into the house where Joseph asked Melinda what she had seen.

"It was too dark to tell if it was a man or animal," Melinda replied.

As the minutes ticked past, the birds and crickets

resumed their songs. When only a gentle breeze stirred amidst the grain, Melinda's pounding heartbeat began to return to normal.

Joseph rubbed his chin. "Could have been coyotes. It's too dark to see anything now. Rascal will let us know if anyone comes back during the night. And tomorrow, I'll take him out to look for tracks."

Pa got up several times during supper to scan the fields. It put Melinda so on edge that she found it hard to sleep when she went to bed. Though she should have been reassured by the watch Rascal was keeping, she could not shake the fear of awaking to find a brave standing over her bed.

She was relieved when it was morning and time to add wood to the stove and put bacon in the frying pan. Melinda knew by Rebecca's bleary eyes that she had fared no better. Melinda took over stirring the eggs while Rebecca stared nervously out the window. "Your Pa went to see if he could find tracks. I hope he doesn't go all the way into the woods."

"How long has he been gone?"

" 'Bout a half hour."

To their relief, they soon saw Joseph striding through the field toward home. Rascal raced ahead, eager for his breakfast.

"Do you suppose he found tracks?" Melinda asked.

"We'll know soon enough."

Joseph frowned as he came into the kitchen. "We found two sets of moccasin prints at the edge of the field. I'm not sure what to make of it. Maybe they were scouts. Were you on the porch when you saw them, Melinda?"

She nodded and shivered, wondering what would have happened if she had not seen them edging closer to the buildings. What had they planned to do? Would they have harmed her family?

She glanced at her mother and saw her exchange a worried glance with Joseph. He put his arm around Rebecca's waist and said, "Whatever they had planned, it looks like you chased them off. Maybe they just wanted a better look at us."

He turned to Melinda. "I want you to keep out of sight for a while."

Melinda suddenly understood the implication of his words and the look that had passed between her parents. Joseph believed the scouts wanted a better look at her, perhaps had even come to find her. He worried that they had heard about an Indian baby who was raised by whites. He had always feared they would come for her someday.

"I'll stay close," she promised.

When breakfast was over, Rebecca turned to Melinda as they cleared away the dishes. "We have company coming in a bit. Maybe you could mix a batch of muffins while I tidy up the sitting room."

"Who's coming?"

In a voice that sounded a little too cheerful, she said, "The ladies of the Missionary Society. Hannah and I have decided to rename the group the Women's War Relief Society. It's our turn to have the meeting. Did you ever finish those mittens you were working on?"

Melinda gritted her teeth "I finished the mittens, but there's nothing in the world that would make me sit through another meeting."

Annie came in for help buttoning her dress. Melinda fumbled with the buttons, and then pulled the sash too tight. Annie protested and Melinda loosened the sash, feeling guilty for taking out her feelings on Annie, who did not deserve to suffer the effects of her churning emotions.

Rebecca studied her, dust cloth in hand. "I know the last meeting wasn't pleasant. Elizabeth Newton seems a particularly snobby girl. But out here, women need one another. It gets lonely if we don't stick together and it would be rude of you to ignore the meeting when you are perfectly able to attend."

Lonely. She had never thought about Rebecca being lonely. Her mother had committed to a difficult life when she left the comfort of Boston society to come West. Though Melinda had never heard her complain, she wondered if Rebecca still missed the life she'd left behind. Maybe that was why she put up with women such as Nellie Anderson. She had little choice with whom she socialized. And though Rebecca might compromise on this point, Melinda had no desire to keep company with the girls from town.

"I could close the door and keep to my room," she offered.

Annie studied her. "Are you sick?"

"No. I'm not sick."

"What shall I say when they ask about you? I won't tell them a lie," Rebecca said.

Melinda sighed. She did not want to put her ma in an awkward position. "All right. I'll come this time because it's here. But I won't go to anyone else's home again."

Rebecca nodded. "That's fair enough. Plan your jam making for our next meeting and I can honestly tell them you are occupied."

Melinda nodded. Yet her mood was not brightened by the knowledge that she would be spared future meetings.

And when Annie cheerfully set about to help her make the muffins, she was irritated by her chatter and could barely hold her tongue when the child spilled batter on the table.

The sounds of buggies coincided with the removal of the baked muffins. Annie displayed them proudly as the women gathered in the sitting room. Rebecca smiled indulgently at her youngest child. "Take one for yourself and sit on the porch with your little sewing kit and work on your stitches."

Nellie glanced at the gathering and said brightly. "With so many of us here today, I think we should send the young ladies into the kitchen to work. They will want to talk about their suitors and will feel more relaxed among one another." She winked at her daughter, who lowered her eyes and pretended to be chagrined.

Since the other young ladies were enthusiastic about the change of location, Melinda was forced to follow along as their hostess, even though she did not feel that she belonged.

Elizabeth chose a muffin and bit daintily into the sweet cake. "I can see why my cousin is so taken with your jams. Your talent must lie in baking. When did you ever find the time to learn?"

Melinda flushed with the unwanted attention. Elizabeth had a way of making her feel like an ant squirming under the toe of her boot.

"I was expected to learn to cook. I suppose you were not," she stated flatly.

Elizabeth laughed as though Melinda had been quite witty. "Oh goodness, no! I was too busy learning how to attract men."

The other girls nodded in appreciation of Elizabeth's

uncontested desirability. Becky turned to her and said, "Speaking of men, I saw you walking down the street with Will Bentley yesterday."

Elizabeth tossed her dark hair. "I like a man who has plans to get out of this town. Since the number of men with ambition is limited, I suppose he'll have to do."

"I hope you already have his heart. He'll be going away in the fall," Susan reminded her.

Her smile was coy. "He's no match for a Southern belle. As I told you, I want out of this town and I've always wanted to see Boston."

Melinda gripped her needles tightly and bit her tongue to keep from ordering Elizabeth out of the house. That anyone could think of Will as a second-rate ticket out of town was inexcusable. Forgetting her usual reserve, she faced Elizabeth squarely and said, "Are you forgetting that he plans to come back here after he finishes his study?"

Elizabeth dismissed the statement with a flick of her hand. "That can be changed."

Becky laughed. "You wicked girl. If anyone could convince him, I'm sure you could. It sure looked that way yesterday. Tell us, what's your secret?"

Elizabeth picked up her knitting. "Flattery, my dear. No man can resist it."

Becky laughed. "You are a naughty girl."

"And clever too. I intend to have a place in society that ensures that Mother and I will want for nothing."

"And your handsome cousin?" Susan asked.

"I don't worry about Parker. He's a sly one. He can take care of himself."

Melinda seethed at Elizabeth's callous use of people.

She longed to run and warn Will. Yet her better judgment told her she dared not mention it to him. Though he had assured her that she was as pretty as Elizabeth, he had not denied an interest in Elizabeth. If he was developing feelings for this shallow girl, she did not want him to think that she was motivated by jealousy. That assumption would destroy whatever relationship was left between them. Hard as it was, she would bite her tongue and hope he would see the truth before it was too late.

The others chatted endlessly, not seeming to notice or care about Melinda's silence. When it was time for them to go, she bid them good-bye and remained in the kitchen as they took their leave.

As she cleared away the crumbs and rinsed the teakettle, she wished that Elizabeth had never come to this town. Yet, wishing would not solve her problem. Elizabeth's presence was a harsh reality that threatened all of Melinda's dreams.

Tears of frustration filled her eyes. She was helpless to protect Will against the lure of Elizabeth's beauty and sophistication. Elizabeth was used to getting what she wanted. And now, she wanted Will.

Yet, Melinda's heart insisted that it had a special claim upon Will. They had been friends for years. And now, dreading the months without him, she would gladly give up her business if he asked *her* to marry him and come to Boston. And she would be going because she cared for him, not because he was a ticket out of town.

She frowned as she remembered Elizabeth's arrogance. Surely there was no truth in it. How would she bear it if Will were to marry the girl right here in their own little church?

Instinct drove her to the coins that lay in her drawer. She fingered them gingerly as she thought about her future. These coins might give her all the comfort to be had. She would watch them grow until they were numerous enough to make her feel secure. In time, perhaps they would even ease the throbbing of a broken heart.

The next afternoon, Eli came to bring more jars and to collect the fresh jam. "Mr. Parker says the combination of your jam and Besse's biscuits are bringing in more business than that old hotel's ever seen. Besse makes the best biscuits you ever tasted."

"I'm sure she does."

"Mr. Parker asked me to fetch you back with me if you'd be his guest for dinner. He says you been helping him out and he hasn't even given you a meal or showed you the hotel. He'd sure be pleased if you'd come."

"Tonight?"

Eli nodded.

Melinda glanced at her dress. "I'll have to check with Ma."

Eli grinned. "I'll wait."

She told Rebecca about the invitation and Rebecca insisted that she go. Though she still felt hesitant, Melinda agreed. After telling Eli, she slipped into her room to examine her dresses. She had only one that might do. It was a soft pastel with puff sleeves and a lace collar. She had never been to dinner at a hotel. She hoped the dress would be fancy enough.

The thought of strange surroundings and an evening with Parker made her stomach churn with anxiety. As she smoothed her hair into a neat twist, she began to wish she had found an excuse not to go. Parker was a man of charm and sophistication. She would feel awkward dining with him. She was sure to make an embarrassing mistake. Yet, she had already told Eli she was coming and had kept him waiting. She would have to go and do her best.

She sat in the front of the wagon with Eli and watched his strong hands guide the team. He chatted amiably about adjusting to the West and his plans for the future. "I'm gonna plant corn and wheat and keep some cattle and pigs. I know how to work fields. I grew up helping my daddy plant and pick cotton. I tell you what, Miss, you ain't worked till you picked cotton. If a man can do that, he can do anything."

When they reached the hotel, Eli parked the wagon. They entered by way of the kitchen. A plump woman stood beside the stove, stirring a kettle. Her dark skin glistened from the warmth of her task. Eli put his arm around the woman and gave her generous waist a squeeze.

"This is my Besse."

She smiled shyly when she saw Melinda. "I'm pleased to meet you. Mr. Parker told me to take special care for your dinner tonight. I hope you like stew. The vegetables come from Eli's garden that he started out back." She nodded to the back of the hotel.

Melinda returned her smile. "My name is Melinda. I'm pleased to meet you too. Stew is one of my favorite foods. Eli tells me you make good biscuits too."

Besse rolled her eyes. "It's been a long time since he's had any others to compare them with." She had a sweet round face and large dark eyes.

"Sounds like you've been cooking since you were young. So have I," Melinda said.

Besse nodded. "I can believe that. Your jam has been so popular we've run completely out. I hope you've brought more."

"We did." Melinda nodded her assurance.

Eli gestured toward a swinging door that led from the kitchen. "I'd best show Miss Melinda to the parlor where she can wait for Mr. Parker. Then, I'll collect that jam from the wagon."

She followed Eli to the front of the hotel where there was a desk and several settees. She seated herself and waited while Eli went upstairs to announce her presence. After a moment, she heard Parker's voice at the top of the stairs.

He descended and stood over her, favoring her with a radiant smile that made her feel like an honored guest. "Melinda, I'm so glad you decided to come. You have changed my prospects of a dull evening to one that I shall enjoy."

She rose and gave him a smile. "It was gracious of you to invite me. However, I never felt that you owed me anything more than the decent wages that you already pay."

"Then, let us call it an excuse to spend the evening in your charming presence. Would you like to have a tour of the hotel? I could explain the many improvements that I have planned."

"Yes. I have only seen the kitchen and parlor. I'd love to see the rest."

"I have not recommended any changes for the kitchen, but I have convinced my aunt to order new rugs for the other rooms. The current ones are quite worn."

Melinda noticed that the rug pattern under her feet had grown dim from years of use. "I'm sure it's been a long time since things have been replaced."

He grimaced. "Wait until you see upstairs. We have ten guest rooms, in addition to our own quarters, all exhibiting the same lack of imagination."

She followed him up to an unoccupied guest room. He opened the door and invited her to step inside. It was clean, yet the bedspread and curtains were faded and the rug was threadbare.

"What would you change about this room?" he asked.

She hesitated while she examined her surroundings. At last she said, "I think a new bedspread with curtains to match would help. And it would brighten the room to get a fresh coat of paint."

He nodded. "I was already planning to have Eli paint the room. Matching drapes and spreads are a good idea. Do you know anyone who could make them?"

He had shown such enthusiasm for her suggestions that she was emboldened to offer her own talents. No matter that she hardly had time to make the jam. She would make the time if she had a chance to increase her savings.

She tempered her offer by stating, "There's a seamstress at the dress shop who could do it. Or, I could make them for you, for that matter."

"Could you? I did not know you could sew, but it does not surprise me. You are a woman of many talents. Perhaps I could see a sample of your work."

"I made this dress," Melinda stated, feeling timid.

She flushed as his eyes skimmed her bodice.

"You did a lovely job. But do you have the time? I would not want you to stop making our jam."

"I have time for both." She pushed away thoughts of the late nights she would spend sewing and replaced them with a vision of coins piled high in a drawer.

"Then it's settled. I know you will do an excellent job. I will pay you a generous hourly wage and you can pick any material you like."

"When would you like me to begin?"

"As soon as you can. If you like, I could accompany you to the mercantile when you come into town again. There are a few things I would like to purchase as well."

They continued the discussion as he escorted her to the dining room. Melinda paused at the entrance, awed by the polished dark walls and round white-clothed tables that were spaced evenly about the room. The aura of formality made her feel like a fish out of water.

Elizabeth and Abigail were seated at a linen-clad table. They rose when she entered and flitted forward to greet her. She hoped with all her heart that they had finished supper and would not be joining them.

Abigail managed a thin, polite smile. "Parker, dear, I see your guest has arrived.

She studied Melinda as though she was assessing an article of clothing, and then said, "I hope you will excuse us. I must see to the dinner menu for next week and Elizabeth has a young man arriving soon to escort her to a social gathering."

Melinda wanted to ask the identity of Elizabeth's escort. Since such a question would be out of place, she replied simply, "I understand."

Elizabeth's eyes were cool as she regarded Melinda. "I'm sure she won't miss us. Parker can be quite charming when he tries."

"Very true, so come along, dear."

Abigail accompanied her daughter from the room while Parker led Melinda to a corner table and pulled back a chair. "I must apologize for my cousin. She is quite spoiled and can be rather shallow at times."

She shrugged. "She's no worse than the children I went to school with."

"I would like to hear about your school days, if you'd like to talk about them, that is."

She puckered her brow. "There's not much to tell. I was an outcast. My mother finally took me out and finished my education at home."

Eli set the stew and hot bread in front of them. When he retired to the kitchen, she looked up to see Parker studying her face.

"Forgive me for staring. While you were talking I realized that you have beautiful eyes. They have charm and expression."

Melinda felt her cheeks grow warm. "Thank you. I can't tell you how many times, as a little girl, I wished for blue eyes and yellow hair."

"You shouldn't have. You're perfect the way you are."

She had heard nearly the same words from Will a few weeks ago. Her heart ached as she remembered the sincerity in his voice, sincerity that she did not assume with Parker.

She brought her wayward thoughts back to him to say, "Thank you. That is very kind."

She glanced around the room. Guests had begun to drift into the dining room for supper. She noticed more than a few curious stares cast in her direction. She tried to ignore them as she sampled the stew.

"Eli had every right to brag about Besse's cooking. This is wonderful," she said.

"She is a good cook, but not much good at running a hotel."

He set his fork down and looked at Melinda. "I've been thinking, since you're going to be spending so much time here, making draperies and bedspreads, why don't you take a room here, at least until you finish the sewing? Then, if you like, you can stay on. I need someone to supervise the housework."

"I thought your aunt and cousin supervised the hotel?"

Parker chuckled. "My aunt is too flighty. She has never had a head for business. It was a wonder she could run her own home. And my cousin fancies herself a Southern belle. She has more important things on her mind than running a hotel, such as how to snare a wealthy man."

Melinda couldn't help smiling at this candid assessment of Elizabeth. She could not imagine Elizabeth taking an interest in housekeeping. Consequently, she was flattered by his confidence in her ability, confidence that was warranted because she had helped Rebecca run their home for years. She knew she could do the job. But what of the expense of taking a room at the hotel? She could not bear to part with the coins collecting in her drawer.

She shook her head. "I don't think I could afford it."

Parker leaned forward. "We have the extra rooms. I certainly would not expect you to pay for your room or meals. I would pay you for sewing and making jam. Promise to give it some thought. It would save a lot of coming and going while you're working on the project."

"It does make sense. I'll think about it."

Dusk had begun to pull its veil over the street when Parker helped her into the buggy to drive her home.

Heads turned as they drove onto the road that led away from town. It was quite a change in style after arriving in the wagon with Eli.

The last rays of sun lingered in an orange haze, bathing the distant mountains in a rosy glow. Parker cast her a glance and said, "I love summer. It's my favorite time of year."

She nodded. "I like the bright green of the trees and the fragrance of flowers."

"You love to be outdoors, don't you?"

"I suppose so. To be honest, my favorite part of jam making is picking the berries."

"Really? Maybe when the Indian threat is over, you can pick your own berries. I'm sure Eli would be willing to give up the job."

They rounded the bend that led to the farm. A rider came toward them. It was Will.

She shrank in the seat, wishing she could hide. What would he think to see her here with Parker?

He drew Ginger to a walk as he reached the buggy.

"Good evening," Parker called, giving him a nod.

"Evening. Nice night for a ride." His eyes were fixed on Melinda.

"I had business at the hotel," she explained.

"She may be working at the hotel soon, helping us run things. By the time I open another one in the South, she might become a part owner."

"Really?" Will's voice was polite but his face registered disapproval.

Ignoring Parker, he spoke to Melinda. "I came by to tell you Sybil had her baby. It's a boy. He looks like Garrett, especially since he doesn't have much hair."

He managed a grin.

News of the baby made her forget her discomfort. "I'll come by and see them tomorrow. Tell Sybil I'm happy for her."

He tipped his hat. "I'll do that. I better get home before Ma worries I've been captured."

They continued their separate journeys. Melinda felt a delirious sense of relief at discovering that Will was not Elizabeth's escort. Perhaps she had turned her attention to another beau. For that, she breathed a profound breath of relief.

Parker pulled the buggy into the farmyard. As he helped her down, she saw Rebecca watching from the kitchen window.

Melinda nodded at Parker. "That was a wonderful dinner. Thank you."

He surprised her by imparting a gentle kiss upon the back of her hand. "Don't forget your promise to think about coming to work. You would be a great help and I would make it worth your while."

Her emotions whirled as she withdrew her hand. His smooth manners made her feel as uneasy as a fly in a spider's web. She would have to be careful and keep her wits to avoid her naïvety being used to his advantage.

"I'll think about it," she promised, as she turned and headed swiftly for the house.

Upon reaching the porch, she glanced back to watch him turn the buggy and head down the lane. The draw of his money was strong. Yet, when she had faced Will in the lane, she had known she could never replace her feelings for him with money. She remembered the disapproval on his face and wished she could have explained the buggy ride with Parker. Perhaps tomorrow she would get a chance.

Rebecca greeted her as she entered the kitchen. "Will was here awhile back. Told us Sybil had her baby."

"I know. We passed him on the road."

Rebecca was silent a moment. Then she said, "Doc came by today after he delivered the baby. He asked if we'd be willing to have some company."

"Who?"

"Adam Smith."

"Why?"

"He's been living with a family in town. He doesn't have any money left to pay them board and he's almost well enough to go home. Pa and Daniel cut some lumber today. They're going to build a little room onto the side of the house for him to stay."

"How long will he be here?"

" 'Bout a month, I'd guess. Maybe two."

"He might like it so well here that he'll decide to stay."

Rebecca chuckled. "Not Adam. He's the independent sort. He'll be aching to get back to his land. At least he'll be close enough here to check on things as soon as he's able."

Melinda didn't look forward to Adam's presence. She knew it was their neighborly duty to take him in. Yet, the crotchety old man had always made her nervous. And though she felt ashamed not to share Rebecca's spirit of charity, she was glad he was staying in a lean-to and not in the house.

She worked late that night, crocheting a set of booties for Sybil's baby until the work began to swim in front of her eyes. When she finally finished, she put down her hooks only to see the unfinished mittens for the war relief lying on the bottom of her work basket like abandoned twins. It bothered her conscience that she had not worked on them for the entire week. She consoled herself with the thought that she had little time to spare after taking on the extra work of making jam. It would take even more time to make drapes and bedspreads. Yet this was work for which she would be paid; pay that she could share with her family.

She awoke late the next morning to the noise of hammers pounding against the side of the house. She lay still and tried to make sense of the sound. Then, she remembered that a small room was to be built for Adam Smith.

She dressed quickly to the smell of bacon sizzling in the cast-iron skillet and biscuits browning in the oven. She hurried to help Rebecca take up the food.

"I'm sorry I'm late. I stayed up to finish booties for Sybil's baby." It suddenly occurred to her that she had never heard the child's name. "What did they name him?"

"Jonathan Garrett Bentley. Nice, isn't it?"

"Yes. Will said he looked like Garrett."

Rebecca smiled. "All relatives think babies look like their side of the family."

"I suppose so."

She mixed eggs and poured them into the leftover bacon grease. She was glad breakfast would be ready soon and Joseph and Daniel would take a break from the incessant hammering that was giving her a headache.

Annie appeared. She set down a plate of butter she had carried from the pantry. "Is all that noise for Mr. Smith's room?"

"Yes, it is." Rebecca handed her some plates to set on the table.

"When is he coming?"

"Tonight, so we'll have to be ready soon."

Annie set the table, and then waited while Melinda fastened her buttons and subdued her hair into two golden braids. Though Annie was independent in many ways, these two personal needs were reserved for Melinda's attention. Melinda was secretly glad. Annie's babyhood had vanished before her eyes. She felt Annie's childhood would go just as quickly.

After they had eaten, Melinda hurried with the dishes and other chores. She was eager to get out to the Bentley place with the gift for the new baby.

Even so, it was afternoon before she was ready to go. She tied on her bonnet and stopped on the porch to show the booties to Ma, who was sweeping. Rebecca glanced nervously across the meadow.

"They're darling. Sybil will love them. But I'm not sure you should walk over there alone."

"We've never seen any Indians during the day. I'll be home well before dark." She was desperate for a chance to talk to Will.

"I guess it would be all right. But don't stay long. Tell Hannah I'll be over later in the week."

Annie tugged at Melinda's skirt. "Please let me come. I want to see the baby."

The women exchanged glances. "I don't mind if she comes," Melinda said.

"Be careful."

Melinda nodded and took Annie's hand. "We will."

She kept a sharp watch as they crossed the field and continued across the meadow. She didn't expect any trouble. Still, she felt relieved when they reached the ranch.

Will was in the parlor holding the baby. He grinned when he saw Melinda. Annie marched right over to hang over the baby and touch his soft cheek with her finger.

Melinda regarded Will thoughtfully. "You fit the part of a doting uncle." And you would make a wonderful father someday, she added in her mind.

"It beats driving cattle to the upper meadow."

"It's a shame you won't get to see much of the little guy when you go away."

"As it turns out, I won't be going quite so soon. Pa asked me to wait till closer to winter. Next spring, he plans to hire another hand. Until I go to Boston, I'll be working with Doc three days a week in town and working three days on the ranch. That way I'll still be learning medicine."

The news that he was staying longer was a mixed blessing. Melinda had hated his plans to leave. Yet, the reprieve would only give Elizabeth longer to win his heart.

Will's face held a guarded expression. "You haven't said anything. Are you glad I'll be here awhile?"

"Yes, of course." She answered honestly.

Before he could question her further, Sybil called from the bedroom. "Is that Melinda? Tell her to come in and talk to me."

Will handed Melinda the baby. "You can take him to Sybil. It's time I got back to work."

Melinda drew a sharp breath. "I'm not sure I remember how to hold a baby. It's been so long since Annie was small."

He laughed. "If I can manage, so can you."

She carried Jonathan into the bedroom where Sybil gave her a sleepy smile. "I see you've met my son. He can't seem to tell night from day. And he's getting spoiled from all the attention. I don't know what I'll do with him when I go back to our home."

Melinda shifted the baby. "I feel awkward. He's so small."

"You should have seen Garrett the first time I handed Jonathan to him. He acted like the baby would break."

Melinda lowered herself into a chair and cradled Jonathan in her arms. "Isn't he cute, Annie?"

"He's awful little."

"Yes, he is. And we brought him a present, remember? Give Sybil the gift I let you carry over."

Annie proudly extended the lumpy, burlap-wrapped package. "Melinda made them."

Sybil untied the package. "Oh, they're perfect. I didn't have time to make any before he was born. Thank you. And the green will match the blanket Elizabeth made."

She held up a neatly crocheted blanket. "She made it yellow and green because she didn't know if I'd have a boy or girl. Isn't it beautiful? She brought it over this morning and even forgave Will for not showing up for a party last night when she heard that's when I'd had the baby."

Melinda swallowed over the lump of disappointment that formed in her throat. Will had been the date Elizabeth was awaiting. And she had been so worried about what he had thought about seeing her with Parker.

As if that was not bad enough, Elizabeth had bested her at a baby gift. Resentment bubbled inside her. Elizabeth had lots of time to spend making the gift since she wasn't busy with chores all day.

"Can I hold him, please?" Annie begged.

Melinda glanced at Sybil.

"If you sit nice and still in the chair, Melinda can put him in your lap," Sybil said.

Annie beamed as she cradled the baby. His tiny face enchanted her.

Sybil, eager for the company of another young woman, continued her chat. "I feel bad Will has had to change his plans about going East," she said. "It's on our account, you know. If we hadn't had that trouble on the ranch we wouldn't be shorthanded. But at least he'll be able to work with Doc. When Elizabeth found out, she offered him a free room at the hotel. Wasn't that sweet? But he already planned to stay with Doc."

The fact that he had not taken the room gave Melinda little comfort. He would be in town three days a week, within easy grasp of Elizabeth's charms. She grimaced. If only he knew what Elizabeth was really like.

She ran her tongue across her lips. "Do you think Will is taken with Elizabeth?"

Sybil puckered her brow in thought, and then shook her head. "He hasn't said a word about her. I'd say she's putting forth more effort with him than he is with her."

Melinda licked her lips that had gone suddenly dry. She tried to muster the courage to ask Sybil if Will had ever spoken of her. But she waited too long. The baby began to whimper and Melinda took him from Annie and set him in Sybil's arms. "He is a beautiful child. You're very fortunate to have him."

Sybil smiled. "I know. Being a mother is the most wonderful experience in the world."

Melinda's heart twisted painfully. Would she ever find out what it was like to hold her own child?

Too quickly, it was time to go. She told Sybil good-bye and herded Annie toward home, determined not to let herself worry about Will and Elizabeth. She would pour her energy into her business. If she was lucky, that would help take her mind off her troubles.

They were halfway across the meadow before she saw the three horsemen. Their long raven braids glistened in the sun. Annie clutched Melinda's skirt. Melinda felt like her feet had frozen to the earth as the men paused to study her, unarmed and with a child.

Chapter Six

Fear gripped Melinda, making her heart melt inside her. Adrenaline raced through her veins, demanding she scoop up Annie and run for all her might. Yet, logic told her that running would not save them. It would take only seconds for the mounted riders to reach them.

Instead, she took Annie's hand and led her along while the trio sat, a hundred yards to her left, surveying them. She kept watch from the corner of her eye as she forced herself to hold her head erect and walk with confidence. Their statue stillness gave her hope that they would respect her courage and not give pursuit.

She glanced down at Annie. Her little face was pale.

They crossed the oat field and entered the farmyard before Melinda dared look back. She was surprised to find that the riders had disappeared as silently as they had come. She released Annie's hand and the child ran calling for Ma. Rebecca was there in a moment. She clasped Annie to her waist while the child babbled incoherently.

93

Rebecca turned a puzzled face to Melinda. "What's she talking about?"

Melinda took a deep breath, still unnerved by the encounter.

"We passed some mounted braves on the way back from the Bentley place."

Rebecca went pale as she scanned the meadow where the girls had crossed.

"They're gone now." Melinda assured her. "They watched us walk home and then disappeared."

Rebecca's voice shook as she replied, "I'm glad you got home safely. The Indians are getting bolder to be out in broad daylight. Your Pa and Daniel went to fetch Mr. Smith. I hope they don't run into trouble."

Rebecca sent Annie to play in her room while they hung the wash. Rebecca's shotgun rested against the tree. She glanced at the fields often, then down the lane. Melinda knew she was not only keeping a lookout, but watching for Joseph and Daniel.

At last, the creak of wagon wheels broke the stillness of late afternoon. The women hurried out to greet the returning men.

"I've been worried sick," Rebecca confided. "Melinda passed some mounted braves on the way home from the Bentleys'. I was afraid they'd be lying in wait for you."

"We didn't see any sign of them. Must have been passing through," Joseph said.

"I'll give 'em a reason to be sorry if I see 'em," Adam sputtered. He raised the rifle from his lap and drew his heavy brows into a scowl.

Joseph frowned. "Put that away, Adam. You won't do any shooting here without my say-so." Melinda could tell

Joseph did not like Adam's sentiments. He remembered too well the unarmed Indian village in his past.

They helped the old man into the house and settled him in a kitchen chair. He continued to scowl as he held his arm stiffly to his side. His fingers rested on his propped rifle in a gesture of security reminiscent of the security blanket Annie had carried for years.

"Fetch Mr. Smith a cup of buttermilk and get one for yourself, if you like," Rebecca told Daniel.

The old man sipped his milk and told a rambling account of the early years of settling his homestead. Daniel sat at his elbow, listening as he described an early skirmish with the Indians when the fort was being built. When the account threatened to become gruesome, Rebecca interrupted. "You have chores to finish before supper, Daniel, and I bet Mr. Smith would like a rest before we eat. Help him to the lean-to so he can lie down for a spell."

Daniel helped the old man to his feet. As he steadied himself on Daniel's arm, he said, "I don't aim to be a burden around here. Adam Smith earns his keep, always has."

Before Rebecca could reply, he shuffled out the door.

Melinda shook her head. "He's a funny old man."

Rebecca nodded. "He's a little rough around the edges. Maybe he needs to be a part of a family for a while."

On Sunday morning, Adam insisted on riding shotgun in the back of the wagon on the way to town. When they got there, he chose to pass his time in the saloon while the family went to church. Rebecca held her tongue regarding his choice. Her forbearance did not surprise Melinda. She knew her mother would wait for the right time to encourage a change in the old man.

At the end of the service, Melinda strolled to the shade of the old willow, the spot where she and Will had always met. She glanced up to see him coming toward her. The smile that he aroused died when she saw Elizabeth watching from the church steps.

Melinda turned away. Self-doubt fueled her tempestuous emotions. Was Elizabeth waiting for him to grace her side like an obedient and well-trained hunting hound? She could not bear to have her think of Will like that.

His footsteps ceased directly behind her. "I was wondering if you'd made a decision about working at the hotel," he said.

Melinda swallowed hard. She longed with all of her heart to throw herself into his arms and tell him that Elizabeth could never love him the way she loved him. Yet how could she do so with the congregation milling around? So she said softly, "Is there a good reason I should not work at the hotel?"

Her tone brought a look of puzzlement. "There could be. How well do you know Parker?"

She turned to face him. Behind him she saw Elizabeth gliding across the lawn toward them.

"About as well as you know Elizabeth," she returned.

He flushed under her steady gaze. "I don't have a right to tell you what to do. But I do worry . . ."

Elizabeth's sugary voice inserted itself into his sentence as she called, "There you are, you handsome man. I was wondering if you'd give me a ride to your ranch. I'd like to pay a call on Sybil."

Melinda's eyes locked on his face. "And I worry too. About you."

She turned abruptly and headed for the wagon where

her family was waiting for her. Joseph helped her on board and they set off to pick up Adam.

When they got home, she helped Rebecca serve cold pork and buttered bread. But her mind was not on the food. She could not help imagining that Elizabeth had been invited to stay for dinner at Will's. Ensconced at their table like a queen, she would put on her best manners and hang on Will's every word. Fear that he would become entangled in her web made Melinda feel sick, for, beneath Elizabeth's pretense of worshipful regard lay a heart of pure granite.

"You don't seem yourself. Is something bothering you?" Rebecca asked when they rose to clear the dishes.

Melinda shook her head. Her mother could do nothing about Will, so she might as well tell her about Parker's proposal. "Parker's asked me to work at the hotel. He's offered me room and board plus extra for my work. Since I'd be making jam and doing some sewing for the hotel, it makes sense for me to live there."

Rebecca's eyes grew wide. "You'd live there with the Newtons? I don't like it." She caught her lip between her teeth as she glanced at Joseph.

Daniel grinned. "I'd like it. We could eat Sunday dinner at the hotel."

"Daniel Pratt, you hush up and take this plate of scraps out to Rascal," Rebecca scolded.

Joseph sat back in his chair and ran a hand across his chin. "I don't know . . . a young girl like you out on your own. It don't seem proper somehow."

"I don't relish living there either. But I'm hoping that if Parker opens a hotel in the South, like he plans, I can stay on and run this one."

Adam shifted with a grunt. "I know I ain't part of this family, but if you don't mind me saying it, there is something to be said about moving this girl to town. Them Indians know she's here and that means danger for the rest of you. No telling what they might do if they have a mind to get her back. Not that I like that dandy who's come to help them fancy ladies run the hotel. Still, it might be best for her to go."

Melinda shivered. She'd never thought about how she might be putting her family in danger. No matter what they said now, her mind was made up. There was no question as to what she had to do.

Rebecca nodded. "Adam does have a point. It would take Melinda out of danger. And whether she likes Parker or not, he does seem a gentleman. I could speak to Abigail about the proprieties."

Joseph studied Melinda. "Is this what you want?"

She nodded.

"Then we'll give it a try. But, first sign of any trouble, you pack your things and come back home."

Melinda nodded. She felt a strange emptiness as she spent the afternoon getting her things together. While she worked, she kept wondering if she was doing the right thing. She would miss her family. Yet there came a time to move on. Maybe this was her time.

When Eli arrived the next morning to pick up the jam, she was ready to go.

"You decided to come to the hotel?"

Melinda nodded. "At least while I'm making the curtains and bedspreads."

"Me and Besse will be mighty pleased to have you there."

"I'm glad to be coming." She swallowed back the lump in her throat. She should be excited to begin this new life. Yet, her heart told her that, in leaving the farm, she was also leaving her dreams. But they were girlhood dreams. She was a woman now and had to think of her future. She would force herself to be grateful that this opportunity had been laid before her.

Annie clung to her skirt as she hugged her family good-bye. She knelt down to the child. "I'll see you every Sunday at church."

Annie began to sob when Eli helped Melinda into the wagon. Melinda watched them until the wagon turned onto the lane. Her last glimpse was of Rebecca, holding Annie, and waving until they were out of sight.

The ride to town was hot and dusty. Eli parked the wagon in back of the hotel and they entered the kitchen. Melinda felt rumpled and sweaty. She was embarrassed to see Abigail, dressed in her finery to go out, standing in the kitchen.

She appraised Melinda. "My dear, I must say I'm surprised. Parker didn't tell me you'd decided to come."

"I just decided yesterday. I hope the job's still open."

"Goodness, yes. You can have the room next to Elizabeth. There's more work around here than either Eli or Besse can keep up with. Eli can bring up your things and you can start right away helping Besse with lunch."

"I didn't bring much with me," Melinda confessed. She felt her face flush as she thought of the trunks of finery that Elizabeth had surely brought West.

"I shouldn't think you will have need of much." With that comment, Abigail sailed out of the kitchen.

Melinda began to help Besse clean a huge pile of beets.

"How many people will be served for dinner?" Melinda asked.

Besse sighed. "Besides the family, there's eight guests and another dozen folk that stop in for meals."

Melinda bit her lip. Helping with large meals each day was more work than she had counted on. She hoped she could still find time to sew and make jam. She consoled herself with the knowledge that she'd never been afraid of hard work. She set her jaw in determination. She would do all they asked and she would do a good job even if she had to stay up all night.

When all the food was set to simmer, she scurried from the hot kitchen for a quick trip to her room. She met Parker coming into the parlor. "Melinda, what are you doing here?"

"I've decided to come and work." She pushed a stray lock of hair behind her ear.

He grinned. "It looks like you have already begun." He took her hand and she felt self-conscious of the beet stains on her fingers. "I am delighted you have chosen to take me up on my offer. I will tell the store to extend credit so you can begin the curtains."

"That would be wonderful. I'm just going up to straighten my things a little before dinner." She was still uncertain if she was expected to help serve. Her uncertainty was put to rest when Elizabeth appeared atop the stairs. She stared down curiously at Melinda.

Parker explained to his cousin, "Melinda has come to do some sewing and help us with the day-to-day running of the hotel."

Elizabeth fixed her with a haughty look. "Then I shall hope the service will not remain so slow."

She turned and disappeared down the hall. Parker released Melinda's hand. "I won't keep you. I do hope you will be happy here."

She forced a smile and said, "I'm sure I will."

She found her room and washed her hands in the rose-embossed basin beside the bed. After arranging her dresses in the wardrobe, she smoothed her skirt and brushed her raven hair. She viewed her reflection in the oval mirror above the basin. Though she looked flushed and hurried, she was presentable.

She hurried down to serve dinner, and then took a quick bite for herself in the kitchen before helping Besse clean up. By the time they finished, it was nearly time to begin supper preparations. With this schedule, she realized she would have to rise before dawn on the mornings she planned to make fresh batches of jam.

The next few days passed in a blur of activities. Still, Melinda managed to squeeze out time to get to the store and choose material for the bedspreads and curtains. Abigail had a sewing machine that Eli moved into Melinda's room and she worked late into the nights sewing the first set of curtains.

By the end of the week, she looked forward to a Sunday rest. She arrived at church and was greeted by her family. Annie was ecstatic to see her, Daniel a bit more reserved. So she hugged them all and joined them in their usual pew.

She felt her heart leap when the Bentley family arrived and seated themselves in the pew behind her. Even though they were feet apart, she was as aware of Will as if he were right beside her. She wondered desperately if she would get to speak to him after the service, or if Elizabeth would interrupt the way she had done the last time they were alone.

Her pulse danced when they were dismissed and she found him waiting for her at the end of the pew. He escorted her to a corner of the church where they were isolated from the crowd that had spilled onto the lawn. As she studied his serious expression, her joy turned to anxiety and she prayed that he would not tell her that Elizabeth had stolen his heart.

She waited, hardly breathing while he cleared his throat and said, "I'm not good at fancy talk like Parker, so I'll just come out and say what's on my mind. You told me once that you didn't care for him, but I'm jealous and I want to know if I've got reason to be. I always thought of us spending our lives together and I don't like the picture of you two that's got stuck in my mind."

She stared into his ruggedly handsome face, the beloved clef in his chin, and his honest brown eyes and she nearly laughed with relief to think that he had been jealous. How many nights had she lain awake lately, agonized by her own jealousy.

She smiled at him and said, "The funny thing is, I've been jealous too. I've watched Elizabeth practically throw herself into your lap and it's eaten me up. You don't have a reason to be jealous because I neither like nor trust Parker. Do I have a reason?"

He grinned, warming her heart like sunshine on a cloudy day. "It seems that we could have saved a lot of misery by telling each other what was on our minds. I don't care a whit for Elizabeth. Sure it was a little flattering at first. Now it's a downright nuisance. Do you really think I could live with a gal like that?"

"I hope not. She is only using you as a ticket out of town. She wants to get to Boston."

He shook his head. "She's worse than I thought."

"I'm so relieved I think my knees are going weak."

Will put his arms around her waist and pulled her against him. "Then let me hold you up."

He enclosed her in his arms, pulling her against his hard, muscled chest. She knew she should pull away before anyone saw them. Yet, a pack of wild dogs would not have induced her to leave the ecstasy of his embrace. He was warm and strong and comforting. She never wanted to part from him again.

He kissed the top of her head. Then she looked up at him, mesmerized by the intensity of his dark eyes as he bent toward her. She knew that he would kiss her and she knew that she had waited all of her life for just this moment. Without a thought of propriety, she closed her eyes and enjoyed the feel of his warm lips upon her own, claiming her softly, promising his heart to her alone.

The sound of buggies leaving the church grounds stole their attention.

Melinda ran a finger along the cleft in his chin and asked, "Is kissing in church proper, Will Bentley?"

He kissed her again, briefly this time. "I can't think of anyplace more appropriate to assure you of how I feel, Melinda Pratt."

She felt as though her heart would burst from her chest from sheer happiness. Will had not been lured by Elizabeth. He cared for her alone. And now that he was reassured that she cared for him, there were no more doubts left between them. And that was the way she intended for it to stay while their friendship blossomed into the full bloom of love.

She would have remained with him forever, marveling at how her fragile dream was coming to life, turning into a reality that she had only dared imagine. All that she had ever wanted was bound up with this man. And now their hopes and dreams were one. He wanted them to be together forever just as she did.

"I want to marry you, Melinda. I've planned on it since we were kids."

Melinda's eyes shone with happy tears. "So have I."

Their intimacy was interrupted when Hannah trod into the church. "Why, there you are, Will. We're waiting on you to come out to lunch."

She smiled knowingly at Melinda. "Could you come too, Melinda? We'd be mighty pleased to have you."

Melinda shook her head. "I wish I could, but I've promised to help serve the noon meal at the hotel."

"Maybe next time," Hannah said. She turned with a grin and walked back to the wagon.

Will walked Melinda from the church. "I'll see you soon, so don't you go takin' up with any fancy Southern men."

Melinda looked into his teasing eyes and said, "Don't you take up with any Southern girls."

He gave her a parting wink and said, "It's a deal."

She told her family good-bye and walked slowly back to the hotel. She could hardly face the rest of the day without Will. She had been sorely tempted to take Hannah up on her invitation. But she had promised Besse her help and she wouldn't break her promise.

She came back fully and painfully to earth when she got back to the hotel and found a room full of hungry customers waiting to be served. Besse's smile, as usual, encouraged her. "I don't know how I ever did this alone. Eli tries to help, but Mr. Parker keeps him too busy with repairs to the hotel. He wouldn't be gettin' any rest today if Mr. Parker were here."

"Where is Parker?"

Besse shrugged. "Don't know, Miss. He has a habit of going away sometimes and not telling nobody where he's been."

Though it aroused her suspicions, Melinda shelved her curiosity and threw herself into the task of carrying out the food.

When Parker returned the next day, he was in a mellow mood. "I see you have settled in," he told Melinda. "You are just what we needed, somebody to run this hotel."

She wished he would hurry and buy the second hotel and move himself and his family to the South. Then she would be free to enjoy running this hotel. Yet she kept this thought to herself and said simply, "I'm glad you think so. I must admit there's lots to do. It will take me longer than I planned to make the curtains."

He put his hand on her arm. The gesture of familiarity made her uncomfortable, yet his expression showed genuine appreciation. "Though I do not want you to be idle, please do not allow my flighty aunt or selfish cousin to work you to death. You come to me if you are ever unhappy."

She nodded and gently drew away. "I will."

She had her first chance to complain the next morning when Elizabeth demanded breakfast in bed during the busiest time of serving. Melinda planned to march straight to Parker. However, her intent became futile when Besse told Melinda that Parker was away again. Since

Abigail never rebuked Elizabeth's demanding whims, it would do no good to appeal to her. So Melinda delivered Elizabeth's breakfast with as much forbearance as she could manage.

When she returned to retrieve the tray, Elizabeth said, "There's a rip in my hem. I shall need it mended before dinner."

The magnitude of the girl's arrogance shocked her. Elizabeth might be used to having slaves do her bidding, but Melinda was not her slave. She was tempted to quit right on the spot and might have done so had it not been for her commitment to her job and her suspicion that Elizabeth wanted her to quit, and was even trying to drive her into that action.

She took the dress without comment and mended it with small expert stitches. She looked forward to the evening. Will had convinced Doc to take their evening meals at the hotel. No doubt Elizabeth planned to wear this dress tonight to impress him.

She found her suspicion confirmed when Elizabeth waited atop the stairs for Will to arrive. As soon as he entered, she strolled down slowly, asking in her sweet Southern drawl if she might join them. And they graciously agreed. The silly charade would have angered Melinda had not Will given her sly winks throughout the meal. In turn, she delivered their meals with polite proficiency and slipped a note to Will telling him just how much he meant to her.

Over the next few days, she found additional consolation in wondering if Will's lack of attention was contributing to Elizabeth's increasingly ill humor. She was sharp with the staff and sullen with her mother. Perhaps she had begun to doubt whether her carefully laid plans for escape were going to be rewarded.

As the weeks passed, Melinda looked forward to stolen moments with Will. And she became used to Parker's frequent absences. Late one evening, when she approached the stairs to begin her weary climb, she heard the front door swing open behind her. Parker entered. His usually tidy hair was disheveled when he removed his hat.

He bowed deeply, if unsteadily. "Good evening, Miss Melinda."

She nodded in return. As he approached, his manner made her apprehensive. He paused beside her and took her arm.

"Shall we go up together?" She could smell liquor on his breath.

When they reached the hallway, he turned to face her. "I believe I owe you your pay. You've done well and you deserve it." He reached in his pocket and drew out several coins.

Melinda cringed. He was speaking too loudly and she was afraid he would disturb the guests. She wished he would lower his voice.

Elizabeth opened her door and peered out at them. She pulled her sleek pink robe about her and stepped into the hall. Ignoring Melinda, she spoke to Parker. "Where have you been, you scoundrel?"

"On business." He bowed in exaggerated politeness.

"Business! You've been drinking. You're just like your daddy. He was a good for nothin' varmint who gambled his money away. And you're no better. What are you going to do when you lose it all? If you think you're getting any of Great-Uncle's inheritance to pay your way out, you have another thing coming."

"Why, my dear cousin, are you under the impression I have been gambling? I would have you know I would never succumb to the fate of my father. I shall soon be far richer than you can imagine and I assure you that I, in turn, do not intend to share it with you."

He turned to Melinda. "You, on the other hand, are a different story. I could be persuaded quite easily to share it with you." He pressed the coins into her hand.

Elizabeth slammed her door, leaving them alone in the hall.

Melinda backed away. Though she was not experienced with men who were drunk, she had heard that liquor could make them do strange things. She could see the truth of that. The man standing before her was not the sophisticated gentleman who had hired her to come here.

Melinda shivered. "I'm tired. I'll be saying good night."

Goose bumps tingled on her neck as she walked to her door. She prayed he would not follow as she stepped inside and turned the key. She felt weak with relief as his footsteps creaked past her door on their way down the hall. Was it only the liquor that had made him act so strangely or was there a dark and dangerous side of Parker? She lay in bed, unable to shake the disturbing thought from her mind.

His apology the next day eased her mistrust. He caught her as she scurried down from sewing to begin dinner preparations. "I got carried away celebrating a business agreement. I hope you can find it in your heart to forgive me. I do not make a habit of acting like a boor."

His dark eyes were earnest as she scrutinized her face. She managed a smile. "We all have bad moments, Mr. Newton. It would be ungracious of me not to forgive."

He followed her to the kitchen where she poured him a cup of coffee. He rubbed his temple and grinned weakly as he accepted the hot brew. "I have a most ghastly headache. I hope this cures it."

He closed his eyes to savor the liquid. When she turned to tend the sizzling bacon, he refilled his cup and drank slowly, leaning his shoulder against the door frame as he watched her move about the kitchen. She felt intensely aware of his presence. Her discomfort from the previous night had not completely faded. She remembered the fear she'd felt when Elizabeth had closed her door, leaving them alone in the hall.

She was glad when Besse joined her. They worked together, laying out plates of eggs in preparation for the bacon.

Parker edged beside her as he set down his cup. "I really want to make up for last night. Will you have dinner with me today?"

"Dinner?" She paused. Her forehead wrinkled into a frown. "I'll need to serve."

He nodded toward the back garden where Eli was pulling weeds. "He can help. He did before you came here."

She shook her head. "I wouldn't feel right, not when there's so much work to do."

His lips curved in amusement. "You are a most unusual and intriguing creature. Most women would jump at the chance to avoid this drudgery. You must learn to think like someone in charge and not like a servant if you want to run my hotel someday."

Melinda bit her lip. His words caused her to have mixed feelings.

He seemed amused with her response. With a chuckle he said, "Get about your work, if that's what you want. I'll see you later."

After he left, she turned to see Besse scowling as she filled the plates. "He'd work Eli to death and not care no more than if he was a pack mule. My Eli has to get up before dawn to pick berries now and still do his other chores."

Melinda was taken aback. "I guess that's my fault."

Besse shook her head. "It ain't your fault. It's his." She nodded toward the doorway where Parker had disappeared. "Better watch out for him. He don't care about nobody but himself."

Melinda picked up a stack of plates and headed for the dining room. Her thoughts swirled in worried confusion. Could she have been so blinded by her own ambitions that she misjudged Parker's character?

She tried to drown her doubts by plunging into her day's work. The curtains for the second bedroom were nearly finished. She planned to start the next set in the morning before making fresh jam. Yet even with her head full of projects, she couldn't shake the feeling that something was not quite right.

To make matters worse, Elizabeth proved to be in a particularly critical mood, putting everyone on edge and bringing her mother close to tears with complaints about the hardships she endured. It was with particular disgust that Melinda witnessed her transformation from tyrant to doting belle when Will came in for a late supper.

Melinda felt his gaze following her as she wiped and

cleared the tables. Once, she glanced up and was amused by the exaggerated long-suffering expression in his dark eyes. She smiled at him softly, assuring him that, whatever he endured from Elizabeth, he still had her love and trust.

When the dishes were washed, she began the ritual of preparing for bed. As had become her habit, she opened her drawer and inspected her money. She fingered the cool coins gently, wanting to gain fulfillment from their growing supply. Yet their cold hardness that she once thought might become her security did not compare with the warm contentment she found in loving Will. Never again would she be able to pretend that money could bring her happiness. For the truth was etched too plainly into her heart.

She closed the drawer abruptly and blew out her candle. She slipped into bed and stared at the ceiling, wondering how much longer she would be alone. For now that she knew Will loved her, she allowed herself to imagine how it would feel to have him cuddled against her each night.

She fell asleep and slept soundly until a knock awakened her just before dawn. Startled, she drew on a worn bathrobe and slipped out of bed. She opened the door a crack and saw Parker. He was dressed in a fresh white shirt and dark vest. He held out his hand and she saw that it held a small wooden box.

"What is it?" she asked.

"Why don't you look inside?"

Her last vestige of drowsiness vanished as she accepted the box and opened the lid. Inside, lay a bracelet of polished stone. She raised her eyes and stared into his face, unable to comprehend the meaning of this gesture. He rose to the occasion with a pleasant smile.

"I still wanted to make up for my bad behavior. I hope you'll accept this as a pledge of my sobriety."

"No. I can't."

"Don't you like it?"

"It's lovely, but I can't take it. Your apology was enough."

He ignored her attempt to return the box. "I'll tell you what. I'll be gone for a few days. You keep it until then. If you still feel the same way, I'll take it back. But I'm hoping you'll change your mind."

He turned and walked away, cutting off her attempt to refuse.

She closed the door slowly and studied the bracelet, touching each polished stone that caught the light in a vibrant spark of color. If it had come from Will, she would have slipped it right onto her wrist. He was the only man whose gift would have meaning. As for this one, she wasn't naïve enough not to know there would surely be strings attached.

She closed the box and placed it into her dresser. When he came back, she would return it. And she would make it clear the relationship they shared would remain strictly business.

Downstairs, Besse was already at work in the kitchen. Her eyes grew wide when she saw Melinda. "Did you hear there was an attack yesterday? I hear a man and his boy were killed."

Melinda's heart lurched. "Who were they?"

Besse shook her head. "I don't know. I heard they live a ways out from town."

Melinda fled from the kitchen and into the street. The first person she saw was the tall figure of the preacher. She caught his elbow. "Please. I heard there was an attack. Do you who was killed?"

He nodded. His lips formed a grim line. "It was the Taylors. Folks in town didn't know them too well, but I was out once with the Doc when the little one was sick. The oldest boy was killed right away and his pa was hurt. His wife brought him to town this morning along with the other younguns but he died before Doc could fix him up. Indians took all but two of their horses."

Melinda pressed her hand to her throat. She had met the Taylors once at the general store. It was hard to believe two of them were dead.

"What will they do?" she asked.

"They'll stay with the Andersons until after the funeral tomorrow. Then they're heading east on the next train."

Melinda thanked him for the information. He walked away, leaving her standing in the road until a passing wagon jarred her from her worried trance. Several families had been already been driven away by the Indians. Would the rest be going soon?

The air was heavy with tension when she served the noon meal. It made her uncomfortable when the talk of Indians stopped abruptly each time she drew near. It wasn't the first time she had been linked with a people she had barely seen and who were poorly understood. It was painful. So, she coped as she had before, by immersing herself in her work.

Several days passed with no more incidents. Parker returned in high spirits a week later. He sent Besse to summon Melinda away from finishing her last set of curtains.

"Mr. Parker wants to see you in the parlor."

Melinda gave Besse a questioning look, but Besse merely shrugged. There was no choice but to go down and see what he wanted.

He was sitting on a settee in the deserted parlor. It was late and the glow of a soft lamp lit his face as he turned to watch her enter the room.

He smiled. "Please, come in. I have been looking forward to seeing you again."

She settled across from him in a straight-back chair. "Did you have a good trip?"

"Excellent. So good, in fact, that I would like to advance your position."

She watched him cautiously and hoped he would offer something she would be able to accept. She saw his eyes drop to her wrist. He frowned. "You are not wearing the bracelet. I had hoped you would consider accepting it as a token of my esteem, for your work, that is."

"I have considered, but I cannot keep it. I haven't done anything to earn it."

He studied her face. "Then I will give you a chance to earn it. I don't feel like waiting for the South to win so I can build a hotel there. Who knows how long the war will last? I am going to California to build my hotel. I want you to come with me."

"You want me to work for you in California?" she asked, trying to think through what he had told her.

"Yes. Things are booming and there's gold to be spent at a good hotel. I want you to share it with me."

She caught her lip between her teeth. How could he believe she would travel a world away from everyone she held dear, especially after what she had seen of his dark side? She drew a long breath. "Thank you, but I don't want to be so far from my family or my future fiancé."

He frowned. "Don't decide too fast. I am offering you a chance you may never get again, a chance to get out of this place. You will have so much money nobody will talk about you the way they do here."

He pulled a bag of coins out of his trouser pocket.

She gasped. "It's a fortune."

"And it's yours just for agreeing to come with me. You're a woman now. It's time for you to leave your family and your farm boy."

He set the bag in her hands, watching her in the unsettling way she had grown to dislike.

She shook her head. "I can't."

He sighed in exasperation. "Don't be a fool. If it's marriage you want, I'll even consider marrying you."

She handed him the bag. She felt calm now, her determination as solid as iron. "I can't marry you. I'll marry Will. And it will be for love, not money."

He shook his head. "Your lack of ambition is proving to be a disappointment. I mistook you for a clever girl who wanted to get ahead."

"I'm afraid you shall have to be disappointed, then."

She turned away. She could feel the presence of his anger as though it was a tangible beast that he struggled to control. His tone when he replied was menacing.

"Think over what I have offered. You may be sorry if you turn me down."

She strode to the stairs. She was shaking when she reached her room. She thought over his words. Had he meant them as a threat? Parker was spoiled, no doubt, and used to getting his way. Yet what could he do if she chose to remain behind? Surely, he was not dangerous. She was letting her fears run away with her.

She tried to put the incident out of her mind. She succeeded on keeping her thoughts on her work and even endured Elizabeth's demands that her breakfasts be brought to her room.

Yet, her patience was wearing thin. Even the coins that she continued to collect in her drawer could not make up for Elizabeth's rudeness or Parker's audaciousness.

The next afternoon brought a welcome caller. She was hanging the last set of curtains when she heard Will's familiar voice. "Besse said I'd find you up here."

She turned to see him standing in the doorway. She was so surprised that she forgot everything except his beloved presence. She flung herself into his arms and was rewarded with a lingering kiss before he held her out and looked at her. "I know you're busy but I had a chance for a break. Do you have time for a walk?"

She gave him a bright smile. "I'll make time. I work hard enough around here to be permitted a break."

He took her hand as they walked along the street and said, "I need your advice. Elizabeth has been getting bolder. She told me last night that I needed a proper Southern wife to start my life in Boston."

He guided her into the shade of a tall piñion and asked, "What should I say to her? Should I tell her that I love you? I don't want to cause trouble for you at the hotel."

He studied her face, uncertainty in his eyes.

"You tell her anything you like. I don't care about working at the hotel."

Delight shone in his eyes. "Really? Then marry me and come with me to Boston."

She swallowed hard, feeling she could not contain her happiness. "I would follow you anywhere. I don't want anything to ever separate us again."

"Neither do I." He caressed her cheek, moving his thumb down to trace her lips.

They lingered together until Melinda said, "I hate to leave you, but I better get back to work. Besse will need help with supper."

"I'll walk you back. And I'll talk to Elizabeth as soon as I get a chance."

After a gentle kiss, they parted at the hotel. Melinda was glad Elizabeth was not hovering at the doorway to see their quick embrace. She knew Elizabeth's disposition and preferred not to be present when Will broke the news.

As she entered the kitchen, she was startled by Parker's angry voice. Eli's eyes were wide as he faced Parker and wiped at the stream of blood that ran from the corner of his mouth.

Chapter Seven

Besse wedged herself between the two men in an attempt to protect Eli. He wiped his mouth with the back of his hand, staring in disbelief at the blood.

Indignant, Melinda cried out, "What have you done?"

Parker spun. His face reflected his struggle for composure. "Elizabeth wanted jam with her biscuits. When there was none to be had, I discovered it was because this lazy oaf has not picked any berries, so Melinda hasn't been replacing what we've used."

He pointed accusingly at Eli.

Eli's dark eyes narrowed. "Asking me to go out there ain't right. Two people just got killed."

"It's not your job to decide what you will or will not do, or to take it upon yourself to stop providing the berries that Melinda needs for the most popular item on the menu."

Melinda stared. She had never met anyone who possessed such a total lack of compassion. It was more frightening than his rage.

118

She struggled to control her temper as she said, "I'm the one who told him not to go out. I thought you would agree that a human life is more important than jam."

Parker turned on her. "He is perfectly safe. The Indians want horses not a worthless brute like him."

Eli's lip had begun to swell. Besse clung to his arm as tears rolled down her face.

"How can you know what the Indians would do?" Melinda demanded. "It's wrong to ask him to chance his life."

"I am not asking him to chance anything, only to do his job. Since he can't seem to do that, he can pack up and get out."

Melinda sucked in her breath. "You can't mean it."

"I do mean it."

By now, Elizabeth had come looking for the jam. She peered into the kitchen. Her smooth forehead creased as she took in the scene. "What is all this shouting about?"

Parker nodded toward Eli. "I will not continue to employ a servant who defies me. He has a choice. He can get in that wagon and go after berries or clear out of here."

"Are you crazy? Who will do the work?" Elizabeth asked.

"Besse. And if she chooses to leave, Melinda can manage until we find more help."

The cold control in his voice made Melinda shiver. She was right to distrust him. He possessed the manners of a gentleman when it suited his purpose. Yet, underneath these smooth manners beat the heart of a cad.

Elizabeth gave a laugh of derision. "Melinda will manage? I wouldn't be surprised to learn that she's in with the

Indians who've been stealing horses. She'll run off and join them one day."

Melinda could not that believe that even Elizabeth would make such an accusation to her face. She had gone out of her way not to offend the spoiled young woman, and received abuse in return. Every instinct told her to lash out, to hurt Elizabeth as she had been hurt. She could tell Elizabeth that Will would not be taking her to Boston, that he had asked Melinda instead. Oh, how she longed to see the look on Elizabeth's face.

Then she thought of Will. He would not know that she had broken the news, would not be prepared for Elizabeth to confront him. So instead, she summoned her restraint, looked into Elizabeth's icy blue eyes and said, "For all your ladylike airs, you are the most ill-mannered and self-ish person I have ever met. I feel sorry for you because you can't possibly be happy."

An angry flush stained Elizabeth's baby-soft cheeks. "My happiness is no concern of yours."

She turned on Parker. "And you have no right to fire any servants. You don't own any part of this hotel. If any-one goes, it's her." She pointed to Melinda.

"It would be my pleasure," Melinda replied. She felt no need to think about this decision. She would pack her things, take her earnings, and walk every step of the way back to the farm if that's what it took to get away from these horrid people. How ironic that they had taken such pains to improve the inside of the building when it was the inward compunction of the owners that needed improvement.

She turned and headed briskly toward her room. She heard footsteps behind her. Parker took her elbow as she reached the bottom of the stairs. "Please, Melinda, don't leave like this."

His voice flowed as sweet as the honeysuckle in a Southern garden. Yet, his Southern charm held no lure for her. She had no doubt there were many charming and honorable Southern gentlemen. Parker, however, was not one of them.

She pulled her arm away. "I've worked hard for you and I believed there was a future here for me. But now that I've seen how you treat the help, I don't want to stay a moment longer. You and Elizabeth are two of a kind, mean as rattlesnakes in your own ways. I couldn't live with myself if I helped you build your fortune. You care for no one except yourself."

His footsteps persisted behind her as she climbed the stairs. At the top of the landing, she turned her to face him.

"Please, Melinda, do not be rash." He struggled to appear conciliatory. "Wait a day or two. Then, if you still want to leave, I will escort you home myself."

"I don't have to think about it. I'll be going back in the morning. However, I may accept your offer of a ride."

He nodded, then replied coolly, "Whatever you wish. I hoped to convince you to reconsider coming with me to California. I see that it is not likely, now."

"I've had an offer of marriage that I intend to accept." The words were out before she considered their potential.

He raised his eyebrows. "Marriage? How interesting. To whom?"

She shook her head. "It doesn't matter."

"I can guess. It's that cowboy, isn't it? Elizabeth has made a fool of herself, forcing her attentions on him. But I've seen the way he looks at you."

His eyes held a cold glint. "What delightful news. I can't wait for my cousin to hear."

"Please don't tell her, not like this." She clasped his sleeve.

He gave a short laugh. "I wouldn't think of it. Just knowing is enough for me, though I believe you are making a foolish choice. He can never give you what I can."

"I don't want what you have."

The anger in his eyes could not be disguised by his smile. "That is your choice. All I ask is that you carefully consider the consequences. I will be going on a trip in the morning. If you decide to leave, my buggy will be at your disposal."

She stared after him as he walked down the stairs. Why had his advice sounded like a warning? It made her uneasy. Yet, she had no choice other than to bear his company a little longer if she wanted to get home tomorrow. She would be glad to be rid of the dark shadow of Parker Newton.

When she had packed, she slipped back to the kitchen to see what had become of Eli and Besse. She found Besse listlessly mashing a large batch of potatoes.

"Did you decide to stay?" Melinda asked.

"Have to. We don't have any money to go anywhere else. Miss Abigail came in and heard what was going on. She says she gave Mr. Parker an allowance to pay the servants, and he says he paid us. But he didn't."

She shrugged unhappily. "Miss Abigail believed him. She says she'll pay me for what I do from now on. Eli's gonna try to find work in town, but what if he can't? He might have to leave me here while he looks for work."

"Where's Eli now?"

Besse nodded. "He went out to the garden. What are we gonna do? He was countin' on that money to get us a place of our own. He found one not far from town. We can't buy it now that Mr. Parker's stole our money."

Melinda bit her lip. Her heart told her what to do. She didn't need her money now that she knew she had Will.

"Come with me," she said.

Besse looked puzzled as she followed her upstairs. Melinda opened her drawer and showed Besse the coins. "You need these more than I do. Use them to get out of here and get a place of your own."

Besse stepped back. "Oh, no. That's your money. I couldn't take that."

"I want you to. I'm leaving tomorrow to go home. I'm getting married, Besse. I won't need the money." Her heart thumped joyfully from hearing her own words.

She filled a worn stocking with the coins and set it in Besse's hand. Tears glistened in Besse's eyes. "This is mighty nice of you, but you know Eli is a proud man. He won't take these."

"I don't want you to tell him until after I've left."

Besse stood uncertainly. "I don't know when we can pay you back."

"It doesn't matter. Just get out of here. You deserve better than this."

Besse wiped away a tear. "Wait till we get our first crop. We'll pay you back. Eli's good at farming. He'll have crops to sell."

"I know he will."

Besse smiled broadly. "I'll hide this under the mattress and tell Eli in the morning. You've made me so happy." She gave Melinda an impulsive hug.

After Besse left, Melinda stared into the empty drawer. She had cherished her treasure so highly and now it mattered so little. Though she could have used it to buy material for a nice wedding dress and new clothes for Boston, a simple dress and her current wardrobe would do just fine.

She felt a deep sense of peace. Letting go of those coins had liberated her from the bitter self-determination to prove herself to this town and replaced it with the satisfaction of helping Besse and Eli. And the thrill of Will's proposal overshadowed all that she had relinquished.

She was relieved that Parker was not present that evening when she helped Besse serve the meal and clean the kitchen. She got to bed early and rose at dawn to join Besse and Eli in the kitchen for breakfast. Eli looked tired from his unsuccessful effort to find work.

"Mr. Parker's going somewhere. His buggy's hitched out front. What you suppose he does when he goes off all the time?" Besse asked.

Eli shook his head. "Up to no good, I'll wager. And no good always comes back on a person."

Parker stuck his head in the door. "There you are. Are you still intent on leaving today?" he asked Melinda.

She nodded.

"It would be my pleasure to give you a ride. And it will give me one last opportunity to convince you to change your mind."

"I won't change my mind, but I will accept the ride." She gave Besse's hand a squeeze. "Let me know when you get settled."

Besse smiled. "You'll be the first I invite for a visit."

Melinda joined Parker in front of the hotel and allowed him to help her into a buggy that was stacked with several valises.

He followed her look of surprise. "I'm heading straight for California. Taking the train to Santa Fe, then continuing by coach."

"Have you told your aunt?"

"Why should I? She is a foolish woman who will soon spend my late uncle's money on her scheming daughter. And Elizabeth will leave her in poverty with no concern for her welfare."

He chuckled softly. "As much as I dislike her, I have to admire Elizabeth. I have no doubt she will go places. It gave me great pleasure to best her this once and leave her short of servants. I like to think of her in the kitchen, forced to sully her lovely hands. She will rise above it, though."

He glanced at Melinda. "You, on the other hand, are a rare unspoiled jewel. It would be a pleasure to give you everything your heart desires, to take you places and spoil you. A woman of your beauty and intelligence could go a long way in a place like California. You could be rich. You could travel and have nice clothes. If you come with me, I'll see that you want for nothing."

She shook her head. "I won't come with you. I could never find happiness in the things you do."

"You are a stubborn woman. I see it would take considerable persuading to make you change your mind."

They rode along in silence until he took the northern fork in the road. She bolted upright in the buggy. "This isn't the way to the farm."

He smiled coldly. A calculating look filled his eyes.

"How perceptive of you, my dear. You are not going home. You're going to meet my partners. If I can't have you, I shall at least make a profit from you."

Panic made it difficult to breathe. "Where are you taking me?"

"Back to where you began. As long as I thought I might have you for myself, I refused to bargain. But you have given me no hope, no reason, to hold you back." His lips curled in a cruel smile.

Dread filled her veins. "Who are your partners?"

"Cheyenne. They want to bring you back where you rightly belong. I offered to meet them near the abandoned mine if you spurned my offer to go to California."

Her thoughts whirled as the ground passed swiftly below them. She could taste the dust that churned from beneath the wheels. She had to stop him before they reached the mine.

As though reading her thoughts, he caught her wrist and held it tightly. "Don't even consider trying to escape. And don't do anything foolish. I want you in good shape when I make the trade."

She jerked and he tightened his grip. "This is not the first time I've traded, you know. They brought me the horses they took from the ranches, in exchange for rifles and whisky. I've sold the horses in other towns for a nice profit."

His confession filled her with revulsion. He had made it possible for the renegades to profit from stealing horses. To that purpose, innocent lives had been lost. And now he was going to California on the money he had made from their blood.

She must get away. Perhaps a surprise blow could

unseat him from the buggy. Then, she could drive back to town and fetch the sheriff. She swung at him with her free arm, striking hard in her effort to free herself and push him off the seat. She struck him again and again.

Startled by her blows, he slowed the team and struggled to grasp both her arms. She saw a line of blood trickle from his lip and felt a primitive satisfaction. He finally pulled the team to stop. With a fierce anger burning in his eyes, he pinned her to the seat with the weight of his body.

"Stop it," he warned. His exerted breath felt warm against her forehead as she fought to free herself. The crushing force of his chest made it difficult to breathe. She began to feel dizzy.

He drew back as the intensity of her struggle waned. "You are not getting away, so you might as well accept your fate."

He pinned her arms and leaned close to her face. His eyes were even with her own. They held a savage light. Immobilized, she tried to quiet her racing thoughts. She needed to think, to find an escape.

"Such a fiery spirit. What a shame to waste it on the Indians. They won't appreciate it like I do."

She jerked aside as he leaned toward her lips. She struggled desperately and almost broke free when his attention shifted to the sound of approaching hoof beats. Then she saw the four mounted Indians. She stared in dread as they drew to a halt near the buggy. The last rider held a string of horses. The men sat tall in the saddle, their raven hair falling down their backs. Parker released Melinda and greeted the brave who rode in front. "Nahkohe, it is good to see you. You have brought fine horses."

"And you have brought the woman," Nahkohe replied. His English was halting, yet clear.

"Yes, just as we agreed."

Melinda gasped. Her eyes locked on Parker in a desperate plea. As much as she disliked the thought of remaining with him, she knew it offered a better hope of escape. If she could convince him to take her to a town, she could refuse to accompany him onto the train.

She clutched his arm. "Take me to the train with you."

His eyes narrowed. "It seems a little late to change your mind."

"You didn't tell me about this. If you had, I would have chosen to come with you."

His brows drew into a frown. "Perhaps that was an oversight on my part. It seems you would choose the cowboy over me and me over the Indians."

A flicker of hope grew in her mind. If she could convince him of his mistake, he might cancel the arrangement and take her. She drew a deep breath. "You don't want to leave me with them. You want me to come with you."

Nahkohe was frowning now. "We have a bargain. You take the horses and we take the woman."

Parker grasped Melinda hard by the shoulders and shook her. "Why couldn't you have come to your senses sooner? Nahkohe is right. We do have a bargain."

The force of his fingers digging into her flesh brought tears to her eyes. "You didn't tell me what you planned to do."

"Bring her here," Nahkohe demanded.

"No," Melinda whispered as she grasped Parker's

sleeve. He made no move to remove her from the buggy. Beads of perspiration glistened on his forehead.

Parker looked up at the Indian. "Let me keep her and I'll come back with rifles and ammunition to pay for her. You can keep the horses."

Nahkohe snorted. "You will take the horses and we will take the woman. She will have children to replace the ones your people killed." He motioned to the rider in the rear and spoke in words Melinda did not understand. The rider dismounted and led the horses forward.

Her heart beat in panic. They weren't going to let her go. She would be carried away to live with a people she did not know.

And no one, not even Will, would know what had become of her. Besse would tell him she had left with Parker. Perhaps he would learn that Parker had boarded a train to California. Would he seek her there?

Nahkohe nudged his horse alongside the buggy. He leaned down, extending his arm toward Melinda. She shrank against Parker.

"Come." He spoke to her. His tone was sharp.

She shook her head.

Suddenly, the buggy was moving as Parker urged the horses forward in an ill-fated attempt to flee. A blast from Nahkohe's rifle shook the air. Parker jerked hard against the seat and slumped. A red stain sullied his white shirt.

The horses raced ahead, panicked by the shot. But they could not outrun the pinto that carried Nahkohe. With the deftness of an expert horseman, he rode alongside the buggy and slowed the horses to a halt. He reached down and jerked Melinda to her feet. She cried out as he used his viselike grip to swing her up to ride behind him as the team of horses ambled away with the buggy, taking her only means of escape.

And so began the longest journey of her life. Nahkohe and his men loped across the open valley, slowing to a walk only when they reached the cover of trees. Bent on escape, Melinda searched the terrain, hoping for a means of rescue. Yet with neither house nor human in sight, she knew her best bet was to keep her sense of direction so that she might escape back on her own.

They rode until early afternoon without stopping. She had left so early in the morning that she'd not bothered with her bonnet. Now the late summer sun beat down mercilessly. Her lips were parched from the heat and dry from the hours she had gone without a drink.

At last, they paused beside a stream. Nahkohe slid from his horse and spoke to Melinda in words she did not understand. He shook his head and made a sound of disgust. "Get down. We will drink and rest the horses."

She scrambled to the stream and cupped the water in her hands. She drank deeply and, when the dryness left her mouth, she glanced at her captors who were joking and tending to the horses. Her heart thudded. Should she chance trying to slip away?

She studied the valley they had left. Buzzards circling in the distance were the only creatures moving above the scorched summer landscape. She watched them dip cautiously to examine their next meal. Sage and juniper stretched as far as she could see. Even if she managed to reach it, she would be hard-pressed to find anywhere to hide. It would be best to go along until she had a better opportunity.

Nahkohe strode up. "Come. We go now."

He mounted his horse and swung her up behind him, brushing aside her full skirt with a disgusted snort when it fell across his leg. Tears welled in her eyes. With every hoof beat, she was being carried farther from home. And though she longed to see Will riding to save her, perhaps it was best he did not know what had happened to her. She could not endure the thought of having him lose his life in the attempt to rescue her.

They rode all afternoon, crossing low hills and winding through arroyos. As the sun moved low in the western sky, they followed a small stream between cliffs that narrowed into a steep-walled canyon. She spotted the teepees of an Indian camp nestled between the walls.

They rode hard for the last mile, arriving amid shouts of greeting. Nahkohe swung from his horse and pulled her down among the women and children who had gathered to inspect the stranger. They fingered her dress, holding the material curiously between their fingers. She wished she could escape their chatter and commotion.

A gray-haired old woman, bent with age, came through the throng. The children parted to let her pass. She studied Melinda and her face crinkled into a smile. She spoke words Melinda did not understand and gestured for her to follow.

They stopped at a teepee with a cooking pot simmering outside the doorway. The old woman filled a bowl and offered it to Melinda, then took another for herself. The aroma of the stew woke Melinda's appetite. She ate quickly, fishing out the chunks of meat with her fingers. By the time she sipped the last of the broth, she felt her strength returning.

The sun was gone, but twilight's glow still provided enough light to see the camp. Families sat grouped around their fires, perhaps fifty in all. A little girl of about three years old wandered over. She held a small slab of meat on a stick. The old woman coaxed her to her lap. She sang softly to the child, who nibbled at her meal and watched Melinda with wide, round eyes. When she had finished the chunk of meat, the little girl grew tired of sitting and wandered away. The old woman clucked softly and spoke to Melinda. She could only guess the woman was explaining their relation. A grandchild, perhaps?

She copied the old woman's example and scrubbed her bowl with sand, rinsing it with a dash of water from another bowl. Then they stacked the bowls together near the doorway of the teepee.

The woman took Melinda's sleeve and drew her inside. A dress of tanned hide lay neatly folded on the floor. She spoke softly and pointed to the dress. Melinda stared at it. The old woman wanted her to change, to put away her identity and become one of them.

She shook her head and the woman frowned. She spoke again more insistently. Melinda heard voices gathering outside the teepee. Perhaps it would not be smart to refuse. It would be easier to escape if she pretended to become one of them. After all, it would take more than a dress to force her to belong.

She picked up the dress. The hide was surprisingly soft. She slipped out of her flowered print and into the Indian dress. As she straightened the skirt, the flap of the teepee opened and a tall young man entered.

Melinda took a step back in surprise and jerked the skirt to her knees. The young man studied her, and then turned his attention to the old woman, whose broad grin revealed several missing teeth.

They chatted while Melinda looked on.

The old woman fetched stew for the man. Then, while he ate, the old woman paraded Melinda, like a prize to be admired, about the camp. She gritted her teeth as the strange language flowed around her. She was surrounded by curious women, some friendly, some looking reticent to accept her.

She was relieved when darkness fell and the families gathered in their tents. Exhausted, she followed the old woman back to her teepee. As they reached the doorway, she remembered the young man. Would he still be there? Her question was answered when they stepped inside. He lay on a bed of skin, sound asleep.

The old grandmother tossed a skin for herself on one side of the teepee and another for Melinda in the center. Then, she wrapped herself lightly and lay down to sleep. Melinda followed her example. Yet she had no desire to sleep. She lay awake, staring into the center hole of the tent.

At last, the camp grew quiet. Even the crickets' night song ceased. She could see a star blinking brightly in the sky. It was the same star that shone above Will and all the people that she loved. Their memory sent tears slipping silently down her cheeks.

Light snoring told her the other occupants were sleeping. She wiped away her tears. Perhaps the chance she longed for had arrived. She crept to the edge of her bedding. If she could make it to the horses she could lead one from the camp and ride all night until she was far away.

She glanced at the sleeping figures. They had not

stirred. She crawled to the flap of the teepee and crept into the night. Her body was damp from anxiety, making her shiver in the gentle breeze.

The horses were tethered up the canyon at the pinon trees. Melinda could hear their restless stirring as she drew near. She slipped silently into their midst and drew her hand along the flank of a sturdy horse. He would do well. She would have to lead him silently away from the encampment before she could mount him.

As she reached into the darkness to unfetter him, someone grasped her wrist. Uttering a terrified gasp, she jerked free and fell hard upon the ground.

Nahkohe stepped from the shadows and loomed over her.

"You have come to help us on a raid?"

He raised his hand as though to strike her. She scrambled backward, scraping the back of her legs against the rocky ground. He laughed as she got to her feet and backed away. Yet his eyes glittered a fierce warning. "Try again and you will be sorry."

She turned and ran for the teepee. Behind her, the horses pounded away to whatever ill purpose they were being ridden.

She ducked inside the flap and fought the sobs that came in great gulps. The old woman awoke and spoke softly, her face full of concern. The young man stirred and turned away.

Melinda curled upon her bed. She could not stop shaking from her fright and the disappointment of her failure. She did not know how long she cried, only that the old woman held her hand, stroking it gently and making a comforting sound until she fell asleep.

She awoke to find the tent empty. She sat up, feeling

bruised and battered. The backs of her legs stung where she had scraped them. She looked out through the door and could see that the sun had already risen. The grand-mother squatted at her fire. She smiled when she saw Melinda.

Melinda stared dully at the wrinkled face. It was kind-ly and she could read concern in the birdlike eyes. Yet, no amount of kindness could erase the gloom that had settled in her heart. Her emotions were spent, leaving her as weak as a rag doll that had lost its stuffing.

The old woman offered her flattened bread. Melinda shook her head. Clucking softly to herself, the woman retreated. No one bothered her again until late in the morning. Then the old grandmother came for her, insist-ing that they join the other women to gather bits of stick for firewood.

The women scattered across the open land, using deer-skin straps to tie up the brush. The small girl she had seen the day before wandered about with them. Melinda noticed the little girl did not stay close to any one of the women and she wondered to whom she belonged.

The sun beat down hot and relentless by the time they started back. The grandmother called to the tiny girl who had begun to lag behind. The child whimpered and reached her arms to Melinda. Melinda hesitated, but a look at the tiny, dirt-smeared face melted her heart. She lifted the child and rested her upon one hip as she carried the bundle of sticks in her arms.

The familiar feel of small arms around her neck reminded her of Annie. She felt a surge of pain at the thought of not seeing Annie grow into a young woman. Would she forget her older sister?

She set the child down when they reached camp. The effort of gathering wood on an empty stomach had left her weak. This time, she accepted the dried meat and flat bread when it was offered. It gave her energy for an afternoon filled with small chores directed by the old woman. She taught by example, shaking her head and clucking softly if Melinda failed to catch on. Yet she remained patient.

As Melinda worked, she noticed that only the old men remained in camp during the day. Perhaps she would rethink her plan of escape. She would pick a time to flee during the day when the old woman was not watching. By the time the young men returned, she would be as far from camp as her endurance would allow.

The young man who shared the teepee returned early in the evening with fresh meat. He watched as she helped the grandmother prepare it for cooking. Ignoring his interest, Melinda kept her eyes on her task.

A commotion in camp prefaced the return of the raiders. They rode in brashly, waving their rifles. Melinda turned away, ignoring their panoply and wondering with whom they traded now that Parker was wounded or dead.

As she walked to the stack of firewood, Nahkohe drew up on his horse. He smiled broadly and said, "I have brought something to show you."

He pulled an ax from the strap on the flank of the horse and dropped it at her feet. She stared in horror at the initials carved into the handle.

Chapter Eight

Melinda had to force her knees to hold her as she faced Nahkohe. "Where did you get that?"

"From the man who held it." He answered in broken English.

His face was cocky, his eyes arrogant. She longed to pound him with her fists. She would have done so if that would change what he had done.

"That's my father's ax. Did you kill him?"

Nahkohe spit onto the ground. "I killed the man who held the ax, but he was not your father. Your father was Indian, like you."

"He was my father. He loved me." Her voice rose, shrill with pain. "What about my family? What did you do to them?"

He dismounted, picked up the ax and replaced it in the strap. Then he looked at Melinda. "I do not kill women and children. But without the man, they will leave. You will have nothing to go back to. Your home is here now with us." He gestured toward the village.

Grandmother was watching, her face creased in puzzlement. Though she could not understand the English words Nahkohe spoke, her eyes held concern.

The young man from her tent, known as Makeeta, began speaking to Nahkohe in the Cheyenne tongue. She did not know what they said, but the tone told her they were arguing. The sight of Nahkohe sickened Melinda. She rushed past him, ran into the teepee, and fell across her bedding. Tears spilled from her eyes as she sobbed for her father and the grief of her family. She longed to be back on her farm where Will could hold her and give her comfort and a reason to live. Would she see any of them again in this life?

Evening shadows darkened the tent and night birds began to sing. Grandmother came in and spoke to her, touching her gently on the arm. Melinda did not acknowledge her and, after a while, Melinda heard the rustle of bedding that told her Grandmother had gone to bed. Melinda lay awake long into the night. Part of her did not believe that Pa was dead. Wouldn't she sense it if he had been killed? And though her tears still soaked into the bedding, she could not completely convince herself to accept his death.

Makeeta did not come into the tent that night. Just before daylight, Melinda awoke to feel someone shaking her shoulder. She resisted consciousness, sensing it would only bring pain. Yet the hand was persistent.

She sat up to see him kneeling beside her. His dark eyes, set above high cheekbones, were urgent. He spoke to her as he took her arm, urging her to rise.

Melinda followed him outside and he squatted in the dirt. He pointed to himself and began to draw a trail with a sharp stick. She puckered her brow as she tried to understand. The trail led to a house. He drew an ax beside it and her heart began to pound.

"My house. You have been to my house?"

He drew the figure of a man as he breathed in and out slowly, so that Melinda could see his breathing. She understood immediately that he was telling her that her father was alive.

Perhaps he thought Nahkohe had lied about killing her father. He must have gone during the night to check. She felt a surge of joy. Then she remembered Adam Smith. Adam was at the house. Perhaps Makeeta saw him and thought he was her father.

She pointed to the figure. "That could be Adam. He's not my father."

She looked into the dark eyes of the young man who had shown such concern for her pain. "Thank you for going for me."

His eyes showed puzzlement. He understood none of her words. She touched his arm gently and tried to smile. "Thank you," she repeated.

He nodded and rose. She watched him stride to the tent. Part of her heart clung to the small hope that her father had not died. Yet, she would never know unless she could see for herself.

When she returned to the tent, Grandmother clucked over her and offered her a bowl of broth. She accepted it, watching the young man eat and wondering if his compassion might lead him to help her escape.

She finished the broth and picked up the stick. She

pointed to herself and Makeeta. Then she pointed to the house. "Would you take me there?"

He frowned and shook his head, uttering a sharp reply before turning away. She bit her lip, hoping he did not think she was ungrateful. No matter. Her family needed her and she was determined to reach them. She would find a way.

Her chance came the next afternoon when the child, Wenaka, had an accident. The women had gone out to collect firewood and Wenaka followed behind, picking flowers and chattering to herself. Suddenly, they heard her cry out. They scanned the rocky canyon. But she was nowhere in sight. Melinda finally found her. She had slipped down the side of a gully. She sat at the rocky bottom, scraped and bleeding and crying as she looked up for help.

Melinda set down the dried juniper she had collected for firewood and climbed over the edge of the bank. The walls were steep and the rocks moved loosely beneath her feet. She gained a toehold and edged herself down the first few feet, setting off a minor rockslide as she slid the last yard to the bottom.

Pebbles bounced against Wenaka's bruised legs and she cried harder, calling for Grandmother who peered over the edge. Melinda inspected her gently and found only bruises and small cuts. She let the child cling to her back so that she would have the use of her arms while she climbed up a spot where a rivulet had worn into the rocky side of the bank. Keeping a precarious balance, she managed a slow climb to the top.

Grandmother took the child and cooed as she inspected her cuts. Then she nodded to the bundle Melinda had dropped, gesturing for her to stay and work while she took the child back to camp. Melinda nodded and picked up the wood. The other women had gone back to their task after seeing that the child was safe. Her heart pounded with the realization that she had another chance to escape. She could work her way down the canyon as she gathered wood. The open brush would be tricky to cross, but after that, she would reach the cover of the cottonwoods.

She fought the desire to cover ground quickly. She would have to give the semblance of collecting sticks so that she did not attract attention. So, she forced herself to move from one scrubby tree to the next until she reached the spot where the canyon wall declined to form a low rocky ridge. She glanced behind her. The other women were not in sight. This time she would escape.

She dropped the sticks and began to run. Once she reached the trees, she would walk all night until she could not take another step. It would take several days to get home on foot and she wanted to put enough distance between herself and the Indians to discourage them from seeking her.

To her right, she saw a flash of movement atop the ridge. Two young women dashed down the slope. They were shouting and brandishing stout sticks. Melinda felt a sickening fear as she realized they meant to intercept her.

She cut to the left, hoping to put distance between herself and her pursuers. She recognized the women. She had seen them the first night she had come to the camp. They were Nahkohe's women. Perhaps he had told them to watch her.

Scrubby plants tore at her legs and cactus thorns pricked her moccasins. She sprinted, driven by panic and heedless of pain. She looked back and saw that they were gaining on her. She tried to run faster, but she was not used to running in moccasins.

She tripped on twisted sagebrush and sprawled onto the dirt. She scrambled to her knees and felt the sharp blow of a stick as it fell solidly across her back. The next blow grazed her head. Dizziness overtook her. One of the women kicked her in the ribs and she curled onto the earth clutching her arms over her head and praying that they would not kill her. The thought of dying before she could find out what had happened to her family was more unbearable than the thought of death.

More blows. More pain. She became less aware as she neared unconsciousness. She heard the sound of hooves, and the beating stopped. Through her dim awareness, she heard a man's voice.

Strong arms lifted her. It must be Will. Will, whom she had always loved and who had always loved her, it seemed. She murmured his name and relaxed, relieved that he had come for her at last. She swayed precariously upon the horse. The landscape spun dizzily around her. Yet he held her tightly.

When they stopped, he lifted her down and carried her to a soft bed. A woman spoke to her. Her tone was full of concern. A damp cloth bathed her face.

"Ma?" Melinda's voice was weak. She squinted at the faces that swam before her.

It was not Will or her mother. It was Grandmother and Makeeta. It was Makeeta who had come to her rescue. The realization that her escape had failed brought a trickle of tears down her cheek and then the blessed peace of unconsciousness.

She slept fitfully, rousing to notice that it was dark

again or sometimes light. Each time she stirred, the old woman offered her a drink and comfort. Once, she awoke to see Makeeta sitting beside her while he finished a new set of arrowheads. She reached out and gratefully touched his arm. He took her hand for a moment and held it gently before he stood and walked off into the night.

She dozed again.

It was daylight when she finally regained her senses. The smell of simmering meat brought awareness of a fierce hunger. She tried to sit up, but movement was difficult. Her back and ribs ached and her legs were black with bruises. Grandmother heard her moving and brought a bowl of meaty soup to restore her strength.

While she rested inside the tent, Wenaka kept her constant company, bringing her treasures of rocks and sticks and chattering in her childish voice. Melinda grew fond of the little girl who sat in her lap and drew pictures in the dirt.

It was two days before she was back on her feet, wobbly at first, then gaining balance as the old woman led her into the sunshine. Her side still ached and her bruises were sore, but she was alive and more determined than ever to find a way to escape.

Soon, she was well enough to go out and collect sticks, wild roots, and berries from squawbush to put in pemmican. The two women who had beaten her were never far away. She sensed they were eager for her to attempt another escape. But she would not make the same mistake. She would wait for an opportunity that afforded no chance for them to catch her.

As the days passed, she began to learn the language. The old woman talked to her often, pointing to objects to help her grasp the meaning. Melinda welcomed the communication. She was tired of her lonely isolation and exhausted by her sense of loss. She learned quickly once she made the effort.

Gradually, the day came when she found it possible to converse with the old woman known as Noa'hehe. Now, she could ask the questions that had formed in her mind. She learned that Noa'hehe was the chief's wife and Makeeta was their grandson. The old chief had taken a small band of braves to hold off a handful of pursuing soldiers when the tribe escaped from the fort. Makeeta was in charge of this camp until his grandfather returned. Unfortunately, Nahkohe and his band were often scornful of his leadership. One morning, Noa'hehe reported a bitter argument between Makeeta and Nahkohe, which had sent Nahkohe storming from camp.

"I worry about Makeeta and Nahkohe. Nahkohe is brave and strong but he does not respect my grandson. Makeeta does not want Nahkohe to trade with white men. He becomes rich and powerful. He makes much for himself but does little for the tribe. I think there will be trouble if the chief does not return soon."

Melinda nodded. "I have noticed Nahkohe and the raiders provide only for themselves while Makeeta and the other young men go hunting to provide for the tribe. I can understand why they quarreled."

"Yes. And also about you."

"Me?"

"Nahkohe would claim you for his wife. Makeeta has claimed you too. You like my grandson, do you not?"

Melinda nodded. "He is a good friend."

"He would make a better husband than Nahkohe."

"He would. But I cannot marry him. Before I came here, I promised to marry another man." She pointed across the canyon toward the great mountain.

Noa'hehe shook her head. "You must forget about him. You must forget about that life. Your life is with us now. You are Cheyenne, like us. This is where you belong."

Melinda did not answer, yet she knew she would not forget. How could she forget when she dreamed of Will every night? And when she arose each morning, she looked across the canyon and wondered if he were thinking of her.

Noa'hehe interrupted her thoughts. "It is Makeeta's right to choose you when the chief gives his blessing. But I think Nahkohe will challenge that right."

The ominous words made Melinda shiver.

She stayed close to the tent as much as possible to avoid Nahkohe and his wives. The insolent way he stared at her bespoke his confidence that, one day, she would belong to him.

Though she was kept busy, the days passed slowly for Melinda. The only time she had to rest before bedtime was a half hour each night when Noa'hehe faced east, rocking on her heels and reciting the soft chant that Melinda recognized as a prayer. Melinda sat nearby, coveting this time alone. It became her refuge as autumn settled into the canyon. The cottonwoods had turned bright yellow and the wildflowers disappeared. The days were shorter and the nights chilly.

Through constant conversation with Noa'hehe, Melinda quickly picked up her native tongue. Little by little, she understood enough to know that Wenaka had a grandmother named Kosa. She was a sickly old woman who rarely left her tent and counted on others to prepare meals for herself and her grandchild. Noa'hehe often undertook the task.

One day, snow began to fall, Noa'hehe asked Melinda to come along to help with the chore. Melinda had grown fond of the child and was happy to do so. She took time to play with her while Noa'hehe helped the bedridden Kosa finish her meal.

That evening, an old man stepped into their tent. Melinda stared, startled by his sudden appearance, while Noa'hehe rose with a cry of joy. His regal bearing made Melinda realize that, in spite of his fatigued face, he must be the chief. His stern gaze fell on her and she wondered what he thought about finding a strange woman in his tent. She also knew that it was his absence that had kept her from becoming Makeeta's wife. Now that he had returned, would he give his blessing?

Makeeta wrapped a blanket around his grandfather's gaunt shoulders and told Melinda, "Heat some stew to warm him."

She stepped outside and stoked the dying fire. Then, she heated the remainder of their supper.

The chief ate hungrily. "There was little to eat on the trail, only a few scrawny rabbits and small game."

Makeeta nodded. "That is all we can find here. Even deer have become scarce."

"We will have to move. We must search for a place where there is buffalo."

He studied Melinda, who was watching him from a corner of the tent, trying her best to shrink out of sight.

"Who is the girl?"

Noa'hehe explained how Melinda had come to them during the last moon and how she had been promised to a white man.

"But she is quickly learning our ways," she added.

The chief frowned. "It was a mistake for Nahkohe to trade for her. If we wish to escape the attention of the white men, we cannot give them reason to come for us."

Makeeta nodded. "That is another reason to move our camp. Nahkohe has heard that white men are searching for her."

Noa'hehe put her hand on the chief's arm. "She was taken from her massacred village by the white man. Yet, she belongs with us. We must not let them find her."

Melinda's heart soared. Will had learned of her escape and was searching for her. Yet, she feared that even if they did not move, he would not find her. With all the narrow canyons winding through this country, it would take a miracle to find the small one in which they hid. Still, if she were never rescued and spent the rest of her life as a captive, she would tuck away this proof of his devotion to sustain her.

Now that the chief had returned, Noa'hehe spent her days making meaty soups to help him recover his strength. Melinda tried to stay out of sight as much as possible. Even though he did not speak to her, his stern presence made her uneasy. On the other hand, when he was not hunting, Makeeta spent his time in the tent listening to his grandfather's tale of the journey.

At the end of the week, the chief called a meeting of the tribe. "I go to search for a new campsite. My grandson will remain to lead hunts for winter food."

He gestured toward Melinda. "When I return, he will marry the daughter stolen from our people."

A murmur filled the camp. Melinda felt the blood drain from her face. Though she had expected the announcement, she had hoped for more time.

Nahkohe spat upon the dirt and strode forward. "What has he done to earn a bride? It was I who took the woman."

The chief's jaw tightened. He turned cold eyes upon Nahkohe. "And taking her may still bring trouble to our camp. But my grandson is pleased with the woman. You should be proud to offer your future chief a gift."

Nahkohe raised a fist. His face held fury. "I am not pleased. Is it right for the weak to steal from the strong? If he wants the woman, let him fight for her. Now. If he can win against me, he will earn his reward."

Melinda's stomach tightened into a knot. Though her regard for Makeeta did not approach her love for Will, she felt a protective fondness for the young hunter who had come to her rescue and shown her kindness. And though he stood several inches taller than Nahkohe, she doubted his agile strength would stand a chance against the hard-muscled power of the older man. She held her breath as she waited to see what would happen.

The chief shook his head. "Your challenge will have to wait until we are settled in another camp. If you do not like my answer, you may take your wives and leave us."

Nahkohe glared at the chief a moment, then turned and stalked away. Melinda let out the breath she had been holding. Like Noa'hehe, she believed that this conflict would not be settled easily and the result might bring disaster to both herself and Makeeta.

She was relieved when Nahkohe left the camp and did not return for several days. When he did, he brought a fine new horse. "I kept this one for myself and traded three others for bullets, blankets, and fur. My wives will be warm this winter."

He eyed Melinda. "You would be wise to hope for a husband who can make your life comfortable."

"I'd rather a husband who did not steal and did not murder innocent people."

"Ha." His laugh was scornful. "You will change your mind when you see who our next leader becomes."

He turned away without waiting for her reply. She stared after him, struck by the familiar words. Hadn't Parker also told her she would change her mind? They were very alike, Nahkohe and Parker, each heedless of anyone else's wishes.

Though she prayed with all her heart that it would not come to a contest between Makeeta and Nahkohe, she knew, no matter the outcome, she could never be happy here. Her heart belonged to one man and she would never give up the hope that they would be reunited.

With the arrival of the bitter cold, the last of the yellow leaves fell from the cottonwoods and the mountains were capped with fresh snow. Game became even scarcer and the women scavenged farther afield for brush and twigs.

Nahkohe's eyes often followed Melinda when he was in camp. When she went out to gather wood, his wives watched for her to attempt another escape. The jealousy that filled their eyes told her it would be worth the beating Nahkohe might give them if they found an excuse to eliminate her from their lives. Melinda knew they would receive no such chance since Wenaka, like an unwitting little guard, trailed behind her as she went about her chores, leaving her no opportunity to slip away.

One evening when she returned the child to her grandmother, Kosa took her hand. Her grip was weak, her fingers cold. Melinda studied the imploring sunken eyes as Kosa said, "I am too old to teach Wenaka what she must learn. I worry about what will happen to her when I am gone. She has come to love you. I hope you will care for her."

Melinda had come to love Wenaka. Yet, she could not promise to stay here because of the child if there was a chance to escape. Nonetheless, if Wenaka needed her, she would care for her in any way she could.

"I will make sure she is cared for," Melinda promised.

The old woman nodded. Her stooped shoulders sagged in relief. She reached a withered hand toward Melinda. "Wenaka's mother was very beautiful. She was much like you. My son loved her very much. They died of a fever while we were at the fort. Wenaka does not remember them."

"I'm sorry."

The old woman's dim eyes clouded with the painful memory. "The fort was a terrible place. It would be better to starve here this winter than to die of sickness and hunger at the fort."

Melinda's heart was burdened by the grief the old woman felt for her dead son and his wife. Whether white or Indian, grief felt much the same. And as she watched Wenaka dig in the dirt as Annie had done, she knew that children, whether Indian or white, were much the same, too.

That evening Makeeta brought a rabbit for their supper. When it was cooked, Noa'hehe told Melinda, "I would like you to take supper to Wenaka and her grandmother. It is too cold out for my old bones."

As Melinda obediently dished up their food, she commented, "Wenaka needs a mother. Kosa is too feeble to care for her and she is on her own too much. Is there a family that would take her in?"

Noa'hehe shook her head. "It is hard to feed another mouth." Many children were left on their own after the sickness at the fort. And many died there."

As Melinda carried meat and bread to the tent, she thought about the suffering these people had endured. Her dark mood lifted as Wenaka spotted her and ran to greet her. Her round dark eyes fixed on the bowls that Melinda carried.

"I have brought food for you and your grandmother. Is she resting?"

Wenaka pushed open the flap and Melinda followed her inside. The old woman lay on her folded blankets. Her white hair flowed from the sides of her gaunt face. Her eyes were dull. She hardly blinked as Melinda set down the food.

"I've brought your supper."

Kosa's lips moved soundlessly.

"Do you have the strength to sit up?" Melinda asked.

Her fingers twitched. But her thin arms would not move.

"I'll help you." Melinda cradled the woman's head in her lap as she put the bowl of broth to her lips. After a few sips, Kosa turned aside, exhausted by the effort.

Wenaka nestled beside Melinda and chewed the flatbread she had been handed. Melinda lowered Kosa gently onto her blanket. There was no doubt she was worse.

"Tomorrow, I will bring more broth."

She glanced at Wenaka who had devoured the bread. She would have to keep a close watch on both of them.

After she had tucked Wenaka into her blanket, she returned to take her own supper with Makeeta and Noa'hehe. "You are sad tonight," the old woman observed.

"I'm worried about Wenaka and Kosa."

Noa'hehe shook her head. "It is the sad way for many of our people."

She looked into the deepening twilight. "It will be worse when it is colder and there is less food. We must soon move to a better hunting ground."

Melinda slept fitfully and awoke to a biting cold the next morning. She drew her worn fur wrap around her before she crawled from her blankets to kindle the cook fire. When she had heated the broth, she filled two bowls for Kosa and Wenaka.

She shivered as she walked over the snow-crusted ground to Kosa's tent. She pushed aside the flap and stepped inside. Her heart sank at the sight that greeted her. Tears ran from Wenaka's almond eyes and down her cheeks. Kosa lay still. Too still.

Chapter Nine

W enaka gazed into Melinda's face with a child's trust that she could make things right. Yet when Melinda touched Kosa's hand, she found it icy cold. She covered Kosa with her blanket before scooping Wenaka and carrying her from the tent. She held her close, wondering how she would explain that her grandmother had died. She contemplated what to say as she hurried through the morning chill to find Noa'hehe.

Noa'hehe was sitting in the teepee, finishing her breakfast. Her eyes filled with sadness at the news. "I knew it would happen soon. Kosa has been sick for a long time."

"I don't know how to tell Wenaka."

"Set her beside me and I will tell her."

Wenaka still clung tightly to Melinda as they sat with Noa'hehe. The old woman reminded Wenaka of the cycles of life she had seen in nature. Wenaka listened carefully and some of the confusion gradually lifted from her face.

"Your grandmother cannot be with you any longer, but she will always love you," Noa'hehe concluded.

Melinda gazed at the solemn child. "She has no family now. I promised to take care of her."

"Then it is proper for you to ask Makeeta's permission. It will be his hunting that will feed her."

Melinda frowned. "He has been providing for her already."

Her answer brought a cluck of disapproval from Noa'hehe. "Makeeta wishes to marry you. You must ask his permission to provide for a child who is not his own."

Melinda had been avoiding the topic of marriage. She did not want to mislead Noa'hehe into thinking her feelings had changed. "I've told you that I hold Makeeta in high regard. But I do not want to marry."

Noa'hehe frowned. "It is foolish to remain stubborn. He will take a wife soon. If not you, then someone else. Then you will have to leave the tent. Who will care for you and the child? Will you hunt the buffalo? Can you snare a rabbit?"

Tears welled in Melinda's eyes at the thought of being forced to marry or condemn herself and Wenaka to starve. She scanned the horizon and yearned for rescue. She longed to go home and end the frightening possibilities of life in captivity. But no one knew where to find her. And they would soon be moving to another camp.

If only she could escape, she could take Wenaka home with her. But in the cold of winter, it would be foolish to try it on foot. And Nahkohe never left the horses unguarded.

She brushed Wenaka's tangled hair from her face and

held her close. If she were forced into marriage, she would not abandon the child. Though others might be willing to care for Wenaka, they could not love her as Melinda did. The little girl might be treated as a second-class member in another teepee. If Makeeta wanted her here, he would take Wenaka also.

Noa'hehe nodded her approval when Melinda sighed and said, "I will ask Makeeta if Wenaka can stay with us."

Her opportunity came late in the morning when he returned with two rabbits in hand. Melinda knelt beside him as he squatted to skin them. "Wenaka's grandmother died during the night."

She waited for his reaction.

His spoke without looking up. "It is no surprise. She was an old woman."

She took a deep breath and plunged ahead. "Wenaka is an orphan now. I would like to ask your permission to keep her and raise her as my own."

He gave her a brief glance. "She may stay. Grandmother is fond of her too."

Gratitude for Makeeta and his generous nature filled her heart. If she had grown up here and never met Will, she could have learned to love him. He would make someone a fine husband. But not her. Her heart belonged to Will.

Later, as the rabbit stew bubbled, Melinda's relief over Wenaka was clouded by Nahkohe's return to camp. He had left days ago after his confrontation with the elderly chief. And though his women had scanned the horizon, their faces tense, as they watched for his return, Melinda had hoped he would never return.

He dismounted from a horse laden with furs and blankets and swaggered to greet his wives. "I have brought you food and riches. And it cost me nothing. The white men were lying near death. Their skin was scarred with disease. I took what I pleased and paid them nothing." He spat on the ground as though disgusted by what he had seen.

"What food have you brought?" The women jostled greedily for a chance at relief from their meager fare.

He pulled smoked meats and cans of beans from a stolen pouch. His eyes located Melinda in the watching crowd. "See what you will have if you become my wife?"

He held up a slab of meat. "Compare this to the scrawny rabbits Makeeta brings to you."

She shook her head in disgust. "At least he doesn't steal to get them. I would never accept anything from a murderer who killed my father for an ax."

Nahkohe walked toward her with an insolent grin. From out of nowhere, Makeeta stepped between them. His eyes glittered with anger. "Our chief will find buffalo. We will follow them and there will be meat for everyone and no one will want what you have stolen."

Nahkohe's eyes narrowed in challenge. "And if he does not return, will you allow us to starve? Or will you lead us back to the fort, to the captivity of the white man?"

Makeeta met the scornful stare. "He will return."

"I would not be so sure. There are soldiers riding the plains in groups of two and three. They have run away from fighting in the white man's war. They kill Indians with no more thought than killing a rabbit. Your grandfather is too old and feeble to fight them."

"He is old, but he is twice the scout you will ever be. He will evade them."

Nahkohe stepped closer. "And you? Are you twice what I am? Or are you a coward? Come face me now and settle the question."

Melinda gasped. She knew Makeeta could not keep the tribe's respect if he were to back down. She held her breath and waited to see what would happen.

Noa'hehe let out a cry. She grabbed at Melinda's arm, lost her feeble grip and crumbled to the ground, still as death.

Melinda knelt beside her.

Attention shifted from the argument to the old woman lying on the ground. Makeeta squatted beside her, patting her wrist and calling her name. When she did not respond or open her eyes, he dismissed Nahkohe's challenge, picked her up, and carried her to her teepee.

He laid her on her blankets, and then sat beside her to call her name until, at last, she stirred. She laid her hand on her heart and said, "I am an old woman. I should be living in peace, watching my great-grandchildren play. Instead, I fear I will see my grandson die."

"When I face Nahkohe, it is he who will die," Makeeta promised.

The old woman shook her head. "Nahkohe is not smart, but he is strong, like an animal. You are smart. You must use your head and be the one to live."

"I will live, Grandmother. And you will live to see your great-grandchildren play."

When he left to go hunting, Noa'hehe raised herself to brush the dust from her clothing. She touched her elbow and frowned. "I fell too hard and bruised myself."

"You should rest," Melinda protested.

Noa'hehe smiled in conspiracy. "There is nothing wrong with me."

Suddenly Melinda understood what she had done. She had created a diversion to break up the fight. No one would think less of Makeeta for ignoring a challenge to care for his grandmother.

Melinda smiled at her. "That was quick thinking."

Noa'hehe sighed. "I will not always be around to stop Makeeta and Nahkohe from clashing. If the chief does not return soon, I fear there will be bloodshed and I could not bear to go on living if Makeeta should be the one to die."

Melinda understood how Noa'hehe felt. There were times she believed she could not go on living without Will or her family. The uncertainty of her father's death lay heavy upon her. She could not bear the thought of never knowing what had happened.

It was fortunate that concern for his grandmother drove Makeeta to pile extra wood on the fire that night. The wind changed to the north and cold air pressed down into the canyon. They found the pot of water in the teepee frozen when they awoke the next morning. Melinda gave Wenaka a blanket to wrap around her as they went to break ice in the creek for fresh water. Even though she knew Wenaka must be cold, the little girl followed stoically behind.

They returned to find Makeeta in conference with the other men. He listened as one said, "We must leave before the winter storms hit or we will starve in this canyon."

Another man shook his head and said, "What about the

soldiers Nahkohe saw? Once we leave the protection of the canyon we will be in the open and likely to be seen. Perhaps we should wait a few more days for the chief to return and lead us to a safe hunting ground.

"And if he does not? We will be too weak from hunger to make the trip. Our women and children will die along the way," insisted the first.

The men turned to Makeeta for a decision. He had been deep in thought as they spoke. Yet now he was decisive. "We will spend two days gathering food and as much meat as we can carry. We will leave the morning of the third sunrise."

"And the chief?" asked one of his council.

"He will find us," Makeeta assured them.

In the afternoon, the sky clouded. The wind blew so cold that Melinda left Wenaka in the tent while she helped Noa'hehe gather food for the coming journey. As they collected the last fall berries and piñon nuts, she considered the consequences of the move. Makeeta had pointed north when she had asked which way they would go. That would take her farther from home.

She had worried over it all afternoon. The steep walls of the canyon not only provided shelter from the wind, but also kept them hidden. Traveling in the open country meant they were likely to be seen. And though she wanted to be seen by Will, being seen and captured by soldiers and taken to a fort would be disastrous. No one would know she did not belong with these people. Would she have a chance to explain? If not, Will might never find her.

Then again, perhaps he might hear about a band of Indians on the move and come looking for her. Her head ached from worry. So, she concentrated on her tasks and tried not to think.

The next morning, Nahkohe roused himself from the drunken stupor that he and his band of raiders had fallen into after indulging in stolen liquor. He had not heard about the decision to move camp. After he beat his wives for packing without his permission, he stormed about the village, saying, "You are fools to move from a safe camp to the open land where you can be found. We can get everything we need by trading with the white men."

Melinda tensed as she waited for the tribe's reaction. Would they follow Makeeta or would their hunger and desperation drive them to agree with Nahkohe?

A young man looked up from where he was hanging meat ready to be smoked. "You would have us become less than men. We would become like mosquitoes, living off others. We do not need the white men. We need to hunt."

"Then you will be massacred. We must trade with the white men and then kill them when their guard is down. Otherwise they will kill us by the hundreds as we walk in circles looking for buffalo that are no longer plentiful."

"We will go far from their towns where they will leave us in peace," spoke one old man.

Nahkohe spat on the ground. "Old fool! They will never leave you in peace. Where will you go that the white men cannot follow? They will hunt you down until the last one among you is dead."

One of Nahkohe's band staggered up. He was shaking and looked ill. Melinda decided it must be the effects of the liquor.

"Are we going with them?" he asked Nahkohe.

"We are not. And neither are my horses."

Nahkohe turned to Melinda. "You would be smart to stay here. We will be warm and will have food for the winter. If you go with them you will die."

She noticed now that, despite his posturing, Nahkohe did not look well either. His flushed face glistened in the frigid air. He took a step, swayed, and caught his balance.

She stepped away from him. "I would rather die than stay with you."

He did not reply, but turned for his tent. Melinda hoped it would be the last she would see of him.

She awoke before dawn on the morning they were to leave. The wind had stopped, but it was bitterly cold. She wrapped Wenaka in a blanket and sat her by the fire that Noa'hehe had started. Then she helped Makeeta dismantle the teepee and prepare to move.

Most of the village was busy preparing for the trip. In contrast to the hive of activity, Nahkohe's women hovered outside his teepee. Low moans rose from inside the tent. Noa'hehe went over to find out what was happening.

"What is it?" Melinda asked when she returned.

"Nahkohe has caught the white man's sickness. His wives are frightened by the blisters that cover his body."

Melinda clutched her blanket more tightly about her. Blisters meant smallpox. Nahkohe had foolishly gone into a camp where men were dying of smallpox. And he had brought it back.

She had seen the ravages it could work on a person. Adam Smith bore the marks on his face. He had been willing to share details about the spread of the disease in the mining camp where he'd worked. She shivered as she remembered his tale of death and disfigurement.

She did not fear for herself. She'd had cowpox as a young girl when she'd taken over the task of milking. Doc Baker had told her it would likely make her immune. But what about Noa'hehe, Wenaka, and Makeeta? Her fear for them made her glad they were leaving camp. They should get away as soon as possible, before others caught the disease. She pulled Wenaka close to her side and wondered how many had already been exposed.

When they departed later that day, Nahkohe and his band were left behind. No one entered his tent to say good-bye. They picked up their packs and hurried away, heading for the mouth of the canyon. The sun shone, but it did not feel warm as they silently made their way onto the prairie. Melinda saw no sign of either soldiers or buffalo as they plodded steadily northward, nor was there any disruption when they made camp near a group of scrubby junipers.

They continued north for several days, living off their provisions and camping where they could find water and shelter from the wind. Then one morning, several people woke with chills and fever, forcing the group to remain at camp:

Makeeta was worried. "Do you know what is wrong with them?" he asked Melinda.

"They have smallpox. Nahkohe carried it back from the white men who were sick."

"Do you know medicine to make them well?"

She shook her head. "We'll have to stay here. It will take a long time for them to get better."

Makeeta nodded as he stared onto the vast expanse that spread before them. He gestured to the plains. "Our food supply is low. I will walk ahead to scout for buffalo. Perhaps meat will help them get well."

She patted his arm, sensing the responsibility he felt for these people. "I will nurse them as best I can. Perhaps they'll be better when you return."

He gathered a small team of hunters. She watched as he led them off on the hunt. Despite his burdens, he carried his shoulders straight. Honor and courage were ingrained in his heart. She respected him and loved him as a brother. She hoped Daniel would grow to be a man she could esteem as she did Makeeta.

She spent the day carrying water from the stream and picking the few berries that survived the frosts. With the little grain she had left, she made a batch of bread. Noa'hehe insisted she was not hungry and left her portion for Wenaka.

The moans that rose from the teepees cast an ominous mood as darkness fell upon the camp. She settled into her blanket and tried to shut out the sounds. As she drifted into restless sleep, visions of scarred faces haunted her dreams.

Early in the morning, Noa'hehe grew restless. Melinda woke and knelt over her, sad to see her shaking with a chill as she clutched her blanket. She bundled Wenaka and carried her from the tent, apologizing when the sleepy child protested against the early chill. Melinda held her against her warm body and spoke soothingly. "Grandmother is sick. We must go and get her some water. Then, you are to stay out of the tent."

When they returned to camp, Melinda cautioned her.

"Remember, you must not come in until Grandmother is well. You wait out here. The fire will keep you warm. Do you understand?"

Wenaka stared at her with solemn eyes. Did she remember when her real grandmother had died? If so, this would not be easy for her. Still, she was a dutiful child and did as she was told.

Noa'hehe's dark eyes were bright with fever. When Melinda knelt beside her, she saw small blisters forming on her face and hands.

"I've brought you water," she said softly. She helped Noa'hehe take a sip. The old woman shook so violently, it was all Melinda could do to keep the cup at her lips. After a moment, she drifted into unconsciousness.

When Wenaka began to cry, she backed out of the teepee and took the tiny girl in her arms. She cradled her silky head and murmured, "It's all right. Everything's going to be all right."

An overwhelming urge to take Wenaka and run from this horror seized her. No one would stop her. In this camp, there was only sickness and death. Yet, even as she thought it, she knew she could not leave Noa'hehe to die of neglect, with no one to bring her a drink or coax her to try and eat. She would stay and do what she could. After all, she could never have borne her captivity had it not been for Wenaka, Makeeta, and Noa'hehe. Still, she must keep Wenaka as far away as possible and hope she had escaped exposure.

When she returned to the stream with Wenaka that evening, a rustling of branches along the bank startled her. She froze, fearing the soldiers. She peered from behind a bush, relieved to find that it was only Nahkohe's favorite horse that had wandered from their former camp.

It still wore a bright blanket as it extended its graceful neck to drink from the stream. She whistled softly and approached, hoping it would not bolt in fear. As she approached, she noticed the dangling reins.

"How did you get here? Did someone ride you?" she whispered.

She glanced around. There was no one in sight except for Wenaka who was busily playing near the water.

The horse watched warily, yet allowed her to get close enough to grasp the leather straps. She tied the horse to a sturdy bush and told Wenaka to stay put. Then, she followed the tracks left in the soft earth. She had not gone far when she saw a figure lying prone on the ground.

She approached cautiously, edging closer until she stood above a woman who lay with her eyes closed, as still as stone. The blisters on her face and hands revealed the cause of death. Melinda recognized her as one of Nahkohe's two wives who had beaten her when she had tried to escape. The woman must have tried to flee the illness by catching up with the tribe. It had been too late for her, perhaps it was too late for those sick in camp. Melinda felt nothing except pity for them now.

She wished she could bundle the body for burial in a tree, as was their custom. Yet she knew she could never hope to lift the woman's body. So she gathered rocks from the gully and piled them atop her. This would forestall predators, at least.

When she hurried back to the stream, she found Wenaka playing upon the bank, unaware of the death nearby. Melinda collected water in the jug, and then led Wenaka and the horse back to camp. She tied the horse where it could graze on clumps of brown grass, then resumed her duty of nursing the sick, many of whom were too ill to raise their heads for a drink. Finally, she fed Wenaka and herself the last of the bread and prayed that Makeeta would return with fresh meat.

He did return that evening as the first stars glowed like candles in the darkening sky. He stumbled toward the fire. On his face, she recognized the first telltale signs of the pox.

"Where are the other hunters?" she asked, helping him into the teepee.

"They fell from the sickness far from camp."

He licked his dry lips and added, "We killed a deer. I dressed it out. The meat is stashed upstream behind a large rock. I carried it until I got too tired."

Melinda nodded. "I will get it. When it is cooked, you will eat and get better."

She knew she dared not wait until morning to get the meat. They needed the food too desperately to chance having it pillaged by a wild animal. So she untied the abandoned horse and led him upstream to a large chunk of granite that stuck out of the streambed. There she found the meat, just as Makeeta had promised, already cut and skinned. She packed it on the horse and brought it back to be smoked. With Wenaka bundled nearby, she added wood to the fire and cooked a large slice of the fresh venison. When it was done, she gave a piece to Wenaka, and then offered some to Makeeta. But he was too weak to eat.

Melinda worked long into the night to smoke the meat. After a short rest, she rose at sunrise to check on the sick. Noa'hehe had died during the night. Melinda pulled the blanket over her body, grieving for the old woman who had been kind and had treated her like a daughter.

Makeeta watched her with fevered eyes. "She is dead?"

Melinda nodded.

He shook violently with a chill. Summoning all the strength left in his body, he said, "You must take the child and leave. Nahkohe's foolishness has brought great destruction upon us. Soon I will follow my grandmother."

"I can't leave you while you're sick and helpless. With my care, you might recover. I know an old man who had smallpox and lived. You are young and strong."

He smiled weakly. "I am not afraid to join my grandmother. If I live, I will miss her."

"I will miss her too. She was kind to me and I came to love her."

She stayed with Makeeta until he lapsed into a restless sleep. Then, she joined Wenaka outside. They nestled near the fire and she felt the child's forehead and studied her smooth skin. Each time she performed the task, she held her breath for fear Wenaka should show signs of the disease. Once again, she released a sigh of relief at Wenaka's cool cheeks and unblemished skin.

They camped beside the fire. In the morning, the camp was eerily quiet. The course of the disease had silenced the moaning, leaving everyone dead or near death. The only people left moving about were herself and Wenaka.

Melinda cut off generous portions of smoked meat for herself and Wenaka. Then, fearful that he had died during the night, she forced herself to check on Makeeta. She called his name softly and he turned to her. Sores covered his formerly handsome face. His lips were dry and cracked with fever.

He whispered hoarsely, "Do you stay only out of pity or do you care for me, just a little?"

Her eyes filled with tears. "You are a fine man. If I had not come here already in love with another man, I would have come to love you enough to become your wife."

He managed to smile. "Then I will die content."

An hour later, Makeeta joined his grandmother. Melinda stood in the doorway as tears coursed down her cheeks. She could have left two days ago. She would have left had it been Nahkohe lying in the tent. But she loved these two people who had become her family.

She wiped away the tears, knowing there was nothing left for her to do. Makeeta had been the last survivor and now he was gone. All that was left was death. This was no place for either herself or Wenaka.

She possessed a fierce desire to put as much distance as possible between Wenaka and this scourge. She gathered their blankets and meat and bundled them onto the horse. She filled the water jugs and tied them beside the meat. As she glanced at the bleak landscape, she was thankful for an animal to pack their supplies.

A dusting of snow fell that morning from a frigid, gray sky. She shivered as she set Wenaka upon the horse and climbed on behind her. She turned the horse south toward the mountains. Home was somewhere near the foothills. She was not sure how quickly they could reach it. Tears blinded her eyes as she thought of her father. And what of the rest of her family? Had they abandoned the place? A vision of a deserted homestead played across her mind.

What would she do if she arrived there and found everyone gone? She dared not think of it anymore. For now, she could only hope a storm would not bury them before they reached safety.

She squared her shoulders and clucked to the horse as they headed into the wind.

Chapter Ten

Now that they had left the camp, Melinda felt the full anxiety of being on her own. Until the onset of smallpox, others had determined her destiny and seen to her needs. Though she had longed for freedom, now that it had come, she felt weighted down by the responsibility for herself and Wenaka. She could not foresee what forces of man or nature she might come against. And there was no one to help her. As the sky darkened like the lid of an iron kettle pressing down upon them, she could only pray that they would be spared the peril of a blizzard.

Late in the afternoon, a light snow began to fall. She scanned the clouds anxiously. They would have to find a sheltered spot where she could build a fire. She had not dared to take extra blankets from the tents because of the threat of contamination. Along with the fire, two thick hides she had brought would have to keep them warm enough at night.

She followed a stream until she saw a spot where a high

bank overhung the shore. It would provide good shelter from the wind and snow. And there was easily enough room for the two of them, along with the horse.

She started a fire with a few dry sticks and then combed the bank for larger branches. By the time she returned, Wenaka was shivering from the cold. Melinda stoked up the fire and settled Wenaka near the blaze. There, they sat together cross-legged, eating strips of smoked venison.

The last of the pale light faded, leaving them enveloped in a cocoon of darkness. "Sleep now," she told Wenaka as she curled next to her. "We still have far to go."

Melinda shuddered when a lone coyote howled. She felt a strange kinship with the loneliness of the cry. She closed her eyes and tucked her chin against Wenaka's soft hair. As the snow swirled beyond the overhang, she took comfort in protecting the child.

Just before dawn, the sound of voices awoke her. There were men on top of the embankment. They must have made camp after she went to sleep. Since they spoke English and not an Indian tongue, she hoped they were someone who would give her aid.

Nonetheless, she decided to be cautious. She was careful not to wake Wenaka as she climbed up to peer through the brush. She held her breath at the sight of two men with scraggly beards and unkempt uniforms. They must be deserters from the war that Nahkohe had warned about. They appeared to be riding along the stream in the same direction she was going. She dared not trust them to be kind if they discovered her.

As she watched, they collected their gear and rode away, leaving her with an uneasy feeling as she climbed back down to Wenaka. She would have to be careful to stay far enough behind these men to keep from being spotted.

She spoke comfortingly as she brushed back the tangles of fine hair that had fallen across Wenaka's forehead. "We're going to play a game. We're going to ride quietly. We won't sing or talk. That way we can hear the song of the birds when they fly overhead. Can you play that game?"

Wenaka nodded and Melinda handed her a piece of dried meat. It was fortunate that Wenaka tended to be a quiet child.

They mounted the horse and followed the stream south. She kept a slow pace to avoid an encounter. Occasionally, she would glimpse the riders on the crest of a distant hill. Then she would guide the horse behind a juniper or piñon and wait until she could no longer see them before resuming the journey.

During the day, the clouds cleared and the sun poured out all its cheerful radiance. They camped at a cluster of boulders that had been warmed by the sun. Melinda was grateful for the stored heat, which allowed them to do without a campfire and risk being spotted.

The next day turned cloudy. When they stopped to camp, she warmed rocks with a fire she made in a tiny crevice and they slept next to the heated rocks. Though she remained cautious to avoid any foolish mistake that would reveal their presence, she began to feel more at ease about the riders, knowing they must be well ahead by this time.

At daybreak, Melinda set their course for the hills. They were less than two days from home. Their journey would take them past the canyon where Nahkohe's greed had spread death among his people. She reined sharply at the sight of a rider at the mouth of that canyon. At first glance, she thought one of Nahkohe's band had survived. But a closer look changed her mind. This rider wore a beard and a dirty uniform. She should have guessed the deserters might find the camp and pause to look for plunder.

The man reached for his rifle, and then narrowed his eyes. She hoped he would choose to ignore them. To her dismay, he shot the rifle into the air. With a whoop, he spurred his horse toward her.

She urged her horse to a gallop and rode hard for the next canyon. Since she could never hope to outrun him while still keeping Wenaka on the horse, her best chance was to put enough distance between them to give her a chance to hide. She rode into the canyon, past vertical walls that narrowed along a stream, pulled the horse to a stop and slipped from its back. She carried Wenaka upstream until the horse was out of sight. If the men followed, perhaps they would take the horse and leave her to finish the journey on foot.

She found a shallow cave for them to climb into and whispered, "We'll stay here tonight."

If the men did take the horse, she and Wenaka would have no food for the rest of the journey. And it would take longer to complete the journey on foot. But it would be a small price to pay if they arrived safely.

Her muscles ached from tension as she strained to hear anyone approaching. Water bubbled along the stream and birds fluttered among the brush. She had just begun to relax when she heard the sound of hooves.

She held her breath, not daring to peer out as footsteps crunched along the bank, sending rocks skittering. Her shoulder blades ached where they pressed against the rocks. Then she saw the bottom of a uniform and a man's face as he bent to stare into the cave. She clutched Wenaka tightly against her as he said, "Well, what have we here?"

He had watery blue eyes and a yellow beard full of dirt. His uniform was faded and torn from lack of care.

His companion asked, "She sick like them dead Injuns in the canyon?"

The yellow-bearded man squatted in front of the cave to get a better look. "She ain't sick. Course it don't matter none to me."

Melinda noticed the craters of pox scars that lay above his beard.

A second pair of shoes appeared and a second man leaned down. He was dark with dirty hair and hard dark eyes. "Think she's one of that tribe of Injuns that sneaked up on us in the canyon?"

"Yup. She's one of them."

"You speak English?"

Melinda did not reply.

The second man glanced behind him.

His friend chastised, "Would you stop being so jumpy? We got 'em all, except her and the kid. Pretty, ain't she?"

He reached for her and she kicked hard at his hand. He withdrew with a scowl.

The other man chuckled. "Ain't very friendly, is she?"

The blue-eyed man said, "Don't matter."

He reached again, grabbing her ankle as she tried to kick. She pried at his fingers, even as she felt Wenaka reach for her, crying in fear as he pulled Melinda from the cave.

He released her so suddenly that she nearly tumbled backward. She stared in shock to see him facedown in the dirt with an arrow in his back. The second man reached for his gun. Before he pulled the trigger, he was pierced by another arrow. He dropped the gun and stumbled downstream, dropping to the ground before he reached his horse.

Melinda choked back a cry as she sought the source of the attack. She recognized the old chief immediately when he stepped from a stand of junipers opposite the creek. His face was expressionless, as though chiseled from stone.

Now that her panic had subsided, she trembled with relief. She regained her senses to hear Wenaka crying in the cave. She lifted her out and held her close.

The chief crossed the stream to face her. His eyes were stern. "You have run away with the child?"

She shook her head, hating to tell him bad news. "The rest of your people are dead. Only Wenaka and I are left."

A flicker of pain passed over his features. "I thought it would be so when I came back from scouting and found death in our canyon."

They were silent until he asked, "My wife and grandson?"

"Their bodies rest two days' ride across the plains." She pointed in the direction from which she had come.

Her eyes fell on the blond man lying motionless at her feet. "You saved our lives. I wish I could have saved your family."

The old man scowled. "These men were in our canyon, looting our dead. My band attacked, but their guns killed my men. I am the only one left."

He reached a trembling hand to stroke Wenaka's ebony hair. "What do you plan to do with her?"

"I promised Noa'hehe I would care for her."

In spite of her gratitude for her rescue, Melinda hoped he would not ask her to surrender Wenaka to his care. As Wenaka tightened her tiny arms around her neck, every protective instinct told her that Wenaka had become her child.

He snorted. "You would take her to the white man's world?"

Melinda nodded. "I must go back. But I will make sure she does not forget her people."

Melinda knew he did not approve. Yet his voice was resigned when he said, "Take her then. Perhaps someday she may return to her people as you did."

His words made Melinda weak with relief. She could not imagine surrendering Wenaka, even though it had occurred to her that she was condemning Wenaka to live between two worlds as she had done. Perhaps she was selfish in holding on to her, for who really knew what was best for the child?

While she was contemplating, the chief turned on his heel, saying, "I go now to bury my dead."

Melinda collected the horse and followed the chief out of the canyon. He held up his hand to stop her as he pointed to a set of riders coming across a distant hill. "There are white men coming this way. Perhaps they are looking for you?"

Melinda studied them cautiously. They were clothed as cowboys, not soldiers.

The chief said, "Go to them. I will wait here until I am sure you are safe."

She rode across the open plain, each yard making her more certain that she had not been mistaken. Her heart pounded. She had dreamed of seeing Will ride to her rescue from the day of her abduction. She shouted his name.

He pulled to a halt with his brother, James, studying her as she rode zealously to meet them. Since she was dressed as an Indian and holding a small child, she wondered when he would recognize her.

Suddenly, he spurred his horse forward. "Melinda!"

They drew their horses to a stop and slid from their saddles. Tears streamed down Melinda's cheeks as they clung to each other.

"I knew you wouldn't give up on me."

She felt his protective arms tighten around her as he nestled his face into her hair. "It's been over a month. I was scared I'd never find you."

"I never stopped hoping to escape. Every day, I imagined I saw you riding to get me. And then, I'd feel frightened for your safety if you did."

He tipped her face to kiss her hungrily. "I'm grateful that it's all over. A deserter told one of the ranch hands there was an Indian camp hidden in a canyon. We've been scouring every ravine, hoping to find you. I'd almost given up. But you're safe now and I'll never lose you again."

He held her out to get a better look, as though afraid she was only a vision. Then his gaze shifted in alarm as he saw the old chief watching from a distance.

Placing his hand on his holster, he asked. "Who's that?"

"The chief. His family died of smallpox and he's all alone."

Her heart twisted with pity at the sad task that awaited him. Her gratitude for his help followed the chief as he turned his horse and rode away.

All this time, Wenaka had sat like a tiny statue atop the horse, staring wide-eyed at the display of enthusiasm Melinda showed for this white man. Melinda lifted her from the horse and said, "This is Will."

"And this one?" Will's curious eyes fixed on Wenaka.

"She's an orphan. Her family died from the pox."

Melinda had forgotten James, who had been patiently observing the scene, until he said, "Now that we've found you, Melinda, we better get riding. We can get a ways before dark and make it home by morning."

Will helped Melinda and Wenaka mount. They rode steadily until the stars sparkled like jewels in the velvet sky. Along the way, Melinda forced herself to ask the question she had been dreading to ask. "Tell me what happened to Pa."

"Your pa?"

She nodded.

"He's fine as far as I know."

Melinda nearly choked on the tears she held back. "Fine? Nahkohe brought back his ax. He told me Pa was dead."

Will chuckled. "It was poor old Adam they got again. He was chopping wood when they raided the farm. Your ma had given him a little pocket Bible. He had it in his pocket and it stopped the bullet. Can you believe it? The Indians took the ax and left him for dead. He was bruised, but he's fine now."

Tears of joy slipped down her cheeks. She began to laugh with such amusement and relief that Wenaka turned to stare at her with grave concern. Melinda hugged the child and said, "It's all right now. Everything's all right."

Since it got dark early in the winter, they made an early camp and heated coffee to wash down their beans and smoked meat. Melinda sat wrapped near the fire, stroking Wenaka's hair until the child fell asleep. When she was sure Wenaka would not awaken, she snuggled against Will until exhaustion overtook her and she fell asleep on his shoulder. When she roused later, she found that she was wrapped in a blanket with Will right next to her, his solid frame keeping her warm.

She awoke early. She could hardly wait to get home and see her family. Now that she knew Pa was alive, her return held no sadness, only joy as she imagined the reunion.

They rode hard and, in the late afternoon, she saw smoke rising from her chimney. She urged the tired horse onward, eager to see what Wenaka thought of Annie and Daniel.

Daniel was in the oat field near the house. He saw them and began to shout and wave his hat. Melinda's heart thumped with such joy that she thought her chest could not contain it.

Rebecca heard Daniel's shouts and came onto the porch. She shaded the fading rays of sun with her hand as she peered toward the riders. Annie stood from churning and clasped her mother by the skirt. And then they were running to meet her. Melinda slipped from the horse and lifted Wenaka down. Daniel reached her first and she clasped him in a hug.

"Wow, you look like a real Indian," he blurted.

Her mother called her name over and over again as she

flew across the farmyard. She sobbed as she clasped Melinda in a tight hug. Melinda closed her eyes and let the tears squeeze out as she rested in the familiar warmth of Ma's embrace.

When she opened her eyes, she saw Joseph running from the barn.

He hugged her tightly. "Melinda! We've been searching for you. I just got back today to get a fresh horse. And now, here you are!"

She wept on his rough homespun shirt. "I'm so glad to see you. I thought you were dead when Nahkohe came back with your ax. But Will told me about Adam."

Joseph laughed. "It made a believer out of the old man."

Rebecca put her arm around Melinda's waist, holding her close, as though afraid she might disappear. "Let's go in the house. You must be tired and hungry."

Melinda glanced beside her and saw Will pick up Wenaka. Wenaka eyed him with suspicion but did not protest. They gathered in the kitchen, where Melinda held Wenaka upon her lap and basked in being surrounded by those she loved. She watched their faces and understood how they had suffered when she disappeared. She would have felt the same sort of loss if the chief had taken Wcnaka from her.

She told the story of how she had come to be captured, her weeks in the Indian village, and her release through the calamity of smallpox. By the time she finished, Ma had supper cooked. Melinda felt her stomach rumble as if awakened from deep slumber. It had been a long time since she had seen a meal like the one being placed before them.

Wenaka ate hungrily, using her fingers to pick up the food until Annie showed her how to use a fork. She was delighted with the new tool and pleased when Annie praised her efforts.

After supper, Annie took her to see her toys. As Rebecca watched them go, she smiled and told Melinda, "She reminds me of you when your pa brought you home to me."

Melinda nodded. She had sat close beside Will all through supper. Now she held his hand. "The whole time I was gone, I kept reminding myself that there was a reason I was there. I had a hard time believing it. Now I know it's true. Wenaka wouldn't be alive if I hadn't been there to take care of her. It's like a repeat of the miracle of how Pa was there for me."

They sat quietly, contemplating and listening to Wenaka's lilting laughter flow from the back of the house. Daniel broke the silence as he happily announced, "Will's going to leave Ginger with me. He can't take her to Boston."

Will smiled at the boy. "Let me give you a word of advice. If you don't want to fall in love, you better not make a habit of taking a pretty girl to school on Ginger's back."

He grinned at Melinda as they all broke into laughter. Then he stood and pulled her to her feet. "Let's go to the parlor."

Melinda glanced instinctively at the dirty dishes.

Ma smiled a radiant smile of sheer joy. "I wouldn't think of having my girl do dishes tonight. You go set yourself with Will and enjoy being safe at home."

They left the kitchen and sat together on the old settee

in the parlor. Will took her hand and turned to face her. "I'm supposed to leave for Boston in two weeks. I want you to marry me and come with me. I can't stand the thought of ever being apart."

Melinda swallowed hard. "All I've ever wanted was to marry you and spend our lives together. But you need to know I can't leave Wenaka behind. I feel she's been given to me as a sacred trust the way I was given to my parents."

He nodded and smiled. "I'd never expect you to leave her. She is your child and she will be my child, just as you were a true daughter to Joseph and Rebecca. And someday she'll be a big sister the way you've been to Daniel and Annie."

She blushed, even as she met his eyes, eyes that were full of love. She basked in his affection and knew that the timid Indian girl who had longed for acceptance was gone forever. In her place was a woman whose experience had given her the grace to befriend those who would accept her and the courage to disregard the rest.

She leaned up to kiss him softly on the lips. "Then it is all settled, Will Bentley. I will marry you and love you forever. Just as I always have."